Douglas B. W. Sladen

Frithjof and Ingebjorg

And Other Poems

Douglas B. W. Sladen

Frithjof and Ingebjorg
And Other Poems

ISBN/EAN: 9783337158217

Printed in Europe, USA, Canada, Australia, Japan

Cover: Foto ©Andreas Hilbeck / pixelio.de

More available books at **www.hansebooks.com**

POEMS

BY

AN AUSTRALIAN COLONIST

FRITHJOF AND INGEBJORG

AND OTHER POEMS

BY

DOUGLAS B. W. SLADEN

AN AUSTRALIAN COLONIST

LONDON
KEGAN PAUL, TRENCH, & CO., 1 PATERNOSTER SQUARE
1882

TO THE

REV. T. W. JEX BLAKE, D.D.

of Rugby School

MY MASTER AND VERY KIND FRIEND FOR SEVERAL YEARS

AND WHO FIRST

BY A JUDICIOUS SELECTION OF POETRY TO READ

TAUGHT ME TO WRITE POETRY

IN GRATEFUL REMEMBRANCE

I DEDICATE THIS VOLUME

DOUGLAS B. W. SLADEN

MELBOURNE
AUSTRALIA
Jan. 1882

CONTENTS.

WATERLOO.

'WHAT struck?'
'Half-past ten o'clock.'
As over his saddlebow he bent
He thought of a village church in Kent,
And said, 'She'll be kneeling soon to pray—
Perhaps for me : it's Sunday to-day.'

'What's that?'
'Oh, a pistol shot.'
Cuirassiers sweeping across the plain.
After them Lifeguards—they turn again.
English beauty is on its knees
For English valour over the seas.

'And those?'
'The van of the foes.'
They've taken the wood by Hougoumont.
Coldstreams and Fusiliers to the front.
Taken again, lads ;—that's not amiss,
Your sweethearts at home will boast of this.

B

Pell-mell
Bullet, shot, and shell
Rain on our infantry thick and fast :
Many a stout heart's beating its last.
Blue eyes will weep for many a day—
Good lives given thus lightly away.

Crash, clash,
With furious dash
Lancer and Cuirassier leap on the square :
Scarcely a third of the bayonets there.
Ye who would see old England again,
'Tis time to prove yourselves Englishmen.

Stamp, stamp,
With its even tramp,
Rolls uphill the invincible Guard :
It staggers at the fiftieth yard,
Weak, worn and oft-assaulted the foe,
Yet never its heart misgave it so.

On, on,
And the fight is won.
Shot-stricken Linesman and thrice-charg'd Guard,
Glares at them hungrily and hard.
His waiting is done—his turn has come ;
Pent-up fierceness drives bayonets home.

On, on,
Lifeguard and Dragoon.
An English charge and a red right-hand
Will bring fair years to your fair old land.
With riven corslet and shiver'd lance
Is reft and shiver'd the pride of France.

Still, still,
In the moonlight chill,
A dying Dragoon looks up to a friend :
' Tell her I did my part to the end ;
Tell her I died as an Englishman should ;
And give her—her handkerchief dipp'd in
my blood.'

There went
From a church in Kent
An eager, anxious prayer to God
For lovers, brothers, and sons abroad :
The fairest and noblest pray'd for one
Not a lover, or brother, or son.

A calm
After hymn and psalm :—
The preacher in silent thought is bow'd
Ere he gives the bidding pray'r aloud.
Hark ! what can that long dull booming be
Swept by the east wind over the sea ?

Boom, boom,
Like the voice of doom.
The preacher has fought, and knows full well
The message that booming has to tell,
And gives out his text, ' Let God arise,
And he shall scatter our enemies.'

One night
In memory bright,
One golden hour alone at a ball,
A kerchief taken—or given—was all.
' Off to the war to-morrow.   Good-bye—
I'll carry it with me until I die.'

' He's dead :
You have come,' she said,
'To give me tidings of him I lov'd ?
Your face has told me your tale—he prov'd
Worthy the name that I did not know,
The man I thought him a year ago.'

' He died,
His sword at his side :
But he liv'd to fight the good fight through :
His last thoughts were of England and you.
He died as an English gentleman should
And sent you—your kerchief dipt in his blood.'

' Ah ! me,
Life is sad,' said she,
' When the sun and sheen of it are gone,'
. And ' one loving heart is very lone ; '
And, ' oh ! if I might lie by you
In your soldier grave at Waterloo.'

EASDALE.

IF e'er thou come to cool Grasmere,
Dear for the dead that held it dear—
Or is it for the greenery
That round about its rim doth lie?—
Fail not to come to Easdale too,
The town upon the hills to view.
'Tis not so wide, or deep, or great
As Windermere or Bassenthwaite :
No islets fringe its little shore,
Like that which floats besides Lodore ;
But in its brown translucent wave
A Dian or a Mab might lave.
   Into its north by-eastern end
Purls a clear beck, whose babblings blend
With the soft bleating of the sheep
Upon the encircling mountain steep.
   All around the lake and vale
Wreathes a mountain-coronal,
Such as Como or Lucerne
Or Maggiore dare not spurn :

Not grey, and gaunt, and giant and bare,
Losing themselves in upper air,
But brave, bluff, hearty English hills
Robed with green and gemm'd with rills,
And overgrown with fern and brake,
Home of our handsome, harmless snake ;
With here and there a boulder-rock
Started by a sudden shock
Of mountain tempest, or left there
When sunder'd from its native lair
By the ice-tide long ago.
    And from the southern end doth flow
The little beck that scarce can fill
In summer heat the Sour-Milk-Gill ;
The river that in winter dances,
Glances, caracoles, and prances,
Most like a charger at his play,
Impatient to begin the fray.
Anon the fray begins ; he flies
Headlong against his enemies.
So not much lower runs the river
And maketh all the hillside quiver.
Well doth it earn its name of ' Force ;'
Such name befitteth well such course.
At last—just so, the battle o'er,
The charger charges on no more ;
But faintly, gently paces home—
So gentlier doth the river come,

Its battle with the mountain past ;
And as the war-worn steed at last
Safe in his stable sound doth sleep,
So doth the river in the deep
Of cool Grasmere to slumber creep.

A BIRTHDAY LETTER.

I.

DEAR sister, 'neath a northern sky
   And on our mother shore,
Another year is fleeting by
   Of your appointed store ;
To-day in England you will end
   A well-spent term again,
And so I snatch a quill to send
   A message o'er the main.

II.

In other days I loved to see
   The smile upon your face,
To hear the laugh of girlish glee,
   And note the kindly grace
Which welcomed with sincere delight
   Each birthday offering,
Alike the jewel and the mite,
   Which Poverty could bring.

III.

To-day beneath a southern sun
   I dream of what has been,
Of dear old days that now are done,
   And each familiar scene ;
Of tea upon the garden-seat
   Beside the leafy limes,
And all the voices that did greet
   My ears in other times.

IV.

To-day between us roll and heave
   Five thousand leagues of foam,
Yet 'tis not easy to believe
   That I am far from home :
For the same friendly English speech
   Salutes the wanderer's ear,
And English hearts and hopes can reach
   This southern hemisphere.

V.

Good-bye, dear sister ! you shall be
   Remember'd well to-night,
We'll drink your health with three times three
   In champagne beakers bright :
Thus ev'ry year, till by and by
   I meet you all once more
'Neath the familiar northern sky,
   And on our mother shore.

FRITHJOF AND INGEBJORG.

Belè, king of Norway, had a daughter Ingebjorg, the fairest of maidens, and a fast friend Thorsten the thegn. Thorsten had a son Frithjof, strongest of men. These two were bred up together in the home of the sage Hilding. They grew and loved each other. Belè and Thorsten died and were buried side by side. Belè had two sons, Helgi, the black-hearted, and girl-face Halfdan. Frithjof coming to them demanded Ingebjorg their sister to wife. Helgi refused. Ring, king of the North, also demanded their sister. Helgi again refused. Halfdan bade him in jest to come and fetch her. Ring invaded Norway. Frithjof being called in to aid the brethren again demanded Ingebjorg in marriage, but in the meanwhile, desiring to see her, violated the temple of Baldur. Halfdan consented, but Helgi once more refused, taunting him with sacrilege.

Frithjof in atonement goes to demand tribute of Jarl Angantyr, but returning finds his homestead burnt and Ingebjorg wedded to Ring. By a mishap he burns the temple of Baldur, and, condemning himself to a lifelong exile on his long ship Ellidè, sweeps the northern seas. Desiring to see Ingebjorg once more, he comes to the palace of Ring in the guise of an old man, but is by him compelled to reveal himself.

The Saga deals of the honour and continence of Frithjof and Ingebjorg, the self-sacrifice of Ring, and the good hap of the lovers.

STILL,

Heedless alike of good or ill,

Sits Ingebjorg by the fire in the hall ;

Beside her sits the Ring, the ruler of all,

Wise and good, and gentle and great ;
To him her will is the voice of fate.
Her love for him is gentle and meek,
She takes his caress and kisses his cheek ;
But sometimes musing as in a dream,
And sometimes wincing as I deem.
And ever and aye she pines away,
Paler and paler day by day :
Every night she sits in the hall
Listening if a foot may fall ;
Every day by the window sill
Watching for one to top the hill,
Still.

Of what thinks Ingebjorg by day,
When she looks to the Southland far away ?
Of what dreams Ingebjorg by night,
Looking at Emberland rugged and bright ?

Can she be longing for eagles' eggs ?
   Queens have had richer gifts than these :
She may have a hundred, if she begs,
   Of any bird by the northern seas.

Ring, the ruler, would joyfully slay
   All the eagles in Norroway creeks,
But for the light of a winter day
   To lure the roses back to her cheeks.

Can she be longing for woodbine bow'rs ?
　Queens may have choicer scents than these :
Magnolia blossoms, and passion flowers,
　And attar of Indian rosaries.

Ring, the ruler, would joyfully seek
　All the odours of all the earth,
To lend his lady rest for a week,
　An hour's content, or a moment's mirth.

Can she be sighing for fell of bear ?
　Queens may ask harder boons than these :
Beast of the field and bird of the air
　Shall die by the thousand if she please.

Ring, the ruler, would joyfully buy
　Every fell in every mart,
To sate the hungering in her eye,
　And draw the aching out of her heart.

Ingebjorg as she sits by the sill,
Watching for farers to top the hill,
Thinks of the woods by her southern home
Where she and one other used to roam.
She was seven and he was eight :
Why should she muse on her little mate ?
Why should she dream of eglantine
And sigh for the scent of wild woodbine ?

When one was seven and she was six,
His tender hands were torn with pricks,
When the reddest rose in the wide wide wood
Was dropped down into her outstretched hood.
Who show'd her the banks where violets grew
Nursed by the leaves and fed by the dew?
Who picked her nuts from the hazel bush
And small wild strawberries sweet and lush?

Ingebjorg as she sits by the sill,
Watching for farers to top the hill,
Thinks of a precipice grim and tall,
And cliff as steep as the castle wall;
An eagle built on its rocky brow,—
Why should she think of that eagle now?
Just where the rock brow ceases to shelve—
She was eleven and one was twelve—
With a coil of rope made fast from his waist
To a rowan-tree on the edge, in haste
While the hungry mother prowl'd for prey—
The father was shot or scared away—
He slid down over the brow and hung
And to and fro with the breezes swung,
And many a fathom down below
A deep and eddying stream did flow.

Danger and death he heeded nought
But only of the eyrie thought,

And seiz'd the eggs and scal'd the rock.
The little maiden knew no shock,
But clapped her hands and ran to grace
The capture at the mountain's base.
He showed his playfellow the best
Of form and warren lodge and nest ;
He decked her out with wing of jay
And wild grebe's breast and many a crest,
And down of finches green and gay.

Ingebjorg as she sits by the sill,
Watching for farers to top the hill,
Thinks of a glen in a wild wide wood
Where she and one—one other—stood,
The best and fairest of his clan,
In years a boy, in form a man,
Save for a narrowness of hip
And silky smoothness of the lip,
In face a girl, in feats a god,
The tops of love and fame he trod.
Her sire was King of all the land
His a poor Thegn at hers command,
But names and grades do little good
When Love meets Beauty in a wood ;
Their words have little meaning now,
But years will give them sense enow.
Now hark ! a noise—that noise again ;
A she-bear charges down the glen.

To shield himself and Ingebjorg
His only weapon is a sword :
He faltered not nor dream'd of fear,
But sword in hand assail'd the bear,
And, spite of hug and rip and bite,
Was winner in the unequal fight.

Ingebjorg, when she sits by the sill,
Watching for farers to top the hill,
Thinks of the bravest in the land
Craving her brother for her hand ;
Of harden'd hearts and pride of place,
Entreaties met with little grace,
And self-sought exile by the side
Of the stern sea's untiring tide ;
Of many a sneer to many a king,
Of Halfdan's message to Ruler Ring,
And rumours of invading spears,
Of Halfdan's folly and Helgi's fears,
Of coasts with foemen overrun,
And homesteads burnt and cottars flown.
And next she sees a maiden placed
In Baldur's temple dread and chaste :
Here might no impious Northmen bide,
Save by the priestfolk purified.
Does she forget how one, who smiled
At the thought of temples being defiled

By the feet of honest men, did scale
At lone midnight the sacred pale ?
Does she forget the bracelet press'd
As token on her willing wrist ?
Or does she deem that Baldur came ?
His beauty well might be the same.
But was the sun-god large of limb
And girt with mighty arms as him ?
The same white flesh might grace them both,
The same clear skin, the same sweet youth.
The sun-god might have hair as gold ;
But was his glance as blithe and bold ?
Does she forget a passion-plight
In Baldur's fane one winter night ?
Does she forget her fear to fly,
Lest she should chafe the god thereby ?
Were she once more in Baldur's fane,
Would sacrilege her feet retain ?
Not, as I think, but that is o'er,
Nor may she dwell upon it more,
Save as a faded golden dream
That once upon her life did beam.
And this is what she muses on,
In her meditation,
Every night-tide in the hall,
Listening if a foot may fall ;
And all the long day by the sill,
Watching for farers to top the hill,
Still.

II.

Grim,
Heedless of eyes that hang on him,
His face half hid by his helmet's rim,
Hand on hilt and tiller in hand,
Sits Frithjof the strongest of the land,
Sick of renown and victory
Won by a willingness to die.
What right has he to live and live
Who wears his life upon his sleeve?
He would fain partake of the mead and song
That flow in Valhalla all day long,
And he would fainer rest with Hel
Than live the life he loved so well
In the morning of years when he play'd
In Hilding's home with the little maid.

The whirlwinds roar and the waves run high
To dash Ellidè against the sky;
The seahill crested, the water shrinks
And thinks to swallow her as she sinks.
Never a word says Frithjof the Strong,
As the stout Ellidè staggers along;
Amid the might and mist of the storm
His eyes are fixt on a woman's form—
Now on the fair-hair'd little maid
With whom a seven-year child he stray'd.

He can well remember the fullest nooks
Where forget-me-nots mirror themselves in brooks :
He can well remember the shady beds
Where blue-eyed violets hang their heads,
And where the firstborn of the year,
The baby primroses first appear,
And where the roses blow their best,
And where around the blackbird's nest
He gathered the choicest buds of May,
And bells of pale campanula,
And ivy leaves, and wove them all
Into a fairy coronal,
And crown'd her queen of forest and fell.
And ever and anon he would dwell
On the twelve-year maid who watch'd him climb
The Norway pines in the brooding-time,
And how she rear'd the wood-pigeon up
He brought unfledged from the fir-tree top ;
And how she call'd from the gorge below
To guide where his feeling foot should go,
When he slid dangling over the edge
To the eagle eyric under the ledge.

Anon on the valley where they stood
When the she-bear bolted out of the wood,
And how he kill'd the bear with his sword
And stripp'd off its skin for Ingebjorg.
She was fifteen then and wept outright ;

She'd have clapp'd her hands at so brave a sight
Three years before : when the fight was o'er
She clung to his side and weeping the more
Smil'd through her tears.   He gave her a kiss,
And after many another I wis ;
He had kiss'd her before but not like this :
Kisses differ one from another
As wife from sister, husband from brother.

   Injebjorg promised to be his wife :
Many a time in her sweet young life
Had she promis'd this, and yet it seemed
So strange that she knew not if she dream'd
Or awoke in Asgard : Frithjof sware
That he would do and he would dare
Deeds that should carry his glory forth
For strength and beauty over the earth.
And stern and bitter waxed he now :
Right well had he fulfilled his vow.
He had wandered over perilous seas
And taken great kings in fortresses ;
Winter and summer, wet and dry,
He had had no roof but the changeful sky.
In the frozen North, tho' the snow fell fast,
When the toils of day were overpast,
He lay on the bare deck glad and grim,
With nought but his shield to cover him ;
He dared the wrath of the southern sun

With fair bare head in an Afric noon ;
He fought in the face of hopeless odds
As if he were indeed of the Gods,
And not an outcast man and accurst,
Longing the bands of life to burst.
He would fight the haughty and the strong,
And spare and shield the weak from wrong ;
He would sweep the seas from East to West,
And North to South, the acknowledged best.
Many a noble maid of the North
With Frithjof the Strong would gladly forth ;
Many a dark-hair'd queen of the South
Would have held the press of Frithjof's mouth
Dearer than ransomless liberty
That he gave in his generosity.
There is not a man in the long dark ship
Would not fainer see a smile on his lip
Than capture the richest argosy
Of Indian gems and spicery.
Frithjof the Strong never smileth now,
But sits and broods on his Viking vow,—
To spoil and slay the haughty and strong,
And spare and shield the weak from wrong.

But in sooth it was not ever so ;
In the golden hours of long ago
There was not a laugh so blithe and long
As was the laugh of Frithjof the Strong,

Whether it was while he did roam
With Ingebjorg in Hilding's home,
Or when he strove in the wrestling ring
With large-limb'd heroes before the king.
But when he thinks on the scorn untoward
And bitter gibe of Helgi the coward,
His face grows wild and white and drawn,
And he longs to pay back blows for scorn,
And writhes to think how he hid his wrath,
And sailed at Helgi's bidding forth
To gather the tribute, right or wrong,
From his father's friend, Angantyr the strong,
And how when he brought the tribute back
There was nothing left but the reek and the rack
Of his pleasant home by the lone seaside;
And how he found that his plighted bride
Was wedded to Ring the ruler of all,
And bode in her husband's northern hall.
Helgi and Halfdan and all their clan
Were sacrificing at Baldur's fane
When Frithjof brought the tribute home.

' Is this my reward when back I come
To find my betrothed another man's bride,
And my long black house by the lone seaside
Burn't down by you ?   Had ye let me bide,
I would have shielded our land from shame,
And sent king Ring by the way he came.

But thou, coward Helgi, come forth and fight ;
When swords do leap forth into the light,
There is little to pick 'twixt king and thegn,
Save what the swords' sharp edge may gain.'

    Down at his feet sank Helgi the coward :
His gibe unjust and his scorn untoward
Prest like a leaden weight on his heart ;
Then Frithjof, stepping a little apart,
Flung the tribute money full in his face,
And stunn'd he lay for a long hour's space.
But seeing the priests advance on him
With daggers drawn and visages grim,
' Now take a simple thegn's advice,'
Said Frithjof, ' lest, thinking to sacrifice,
Ye be the victims yourselves to-day,
Ye wool-clad throng.'   And they shrank away.

    When Frithjof saw the bracelet he press'd
On his plighting night on Ingebjorg's wrist,
On the wooden arm of the summer-god,
Then straightway up to the image he strode
And pluck'd it off : yet so fast it held
That, while he was wrenching it off, he fell'd
The image of Baldur into the fire.
The flames rose higher and higher and higher,
And licking the shields that roofed the fane,
Shower'd down the gold in a golden rain,

And the lurid morning dawn'd upon
Smouldering ember and calcin'd stone.
Then Frithjof sail'd out to sea once more,
More weary of living than before ;
And all men held him accurst of heaven,
And they looked to see Ellidè riven
By the thunder of Thor or Odin's hand.
But Frithjof push'd unscath'd from the strand,
And swept the seas throughout three long years ;
Hopeless of hopes and fearless of fears,
Slaying and spoiling the haughty and strong,
And sparing and shielding the weak from wrong.
Nor car'd he for aught save victory,
And, when victorious, long'd to die ;
Striving to wander and sail away
From the hungry wakeful wish that lay
In the safest, deepest nook of his heart,
Unwilling to die or to depart.
And to-day the wish is strongest of all
To steal into Ring the Ruler's hall,
Disguis'd from the gaze of friendly ken,
To look upon Ingebjorg again—
And die.
Then he push'd back his helmet wearily
And turning the ship's head toward the strand,
The mariners hail'd on either hand :
Vikings, pull merrily, merrily ;
To-day we make the land.

III.

Still,
Heedless alike of good and of ill,
Sits Ingebjorg by the fire in the hall;
Beside her sits Ring the ruler of all.
She grows paler and paler day by day;
Her tide is ever ebbing away,—
Listless and feeble and gentle and meek—
No spring in her gait, no may in her cheek.

Outside the winter is rough to-night,
Inside the beech logs burn brisk and bright;
Below the dais, in rude content,
Or roystering boisterous merriment,
Sing henchmen and thingmen mirthfully.

No glimmer of light is in her eye,
Save when she hears a foot on the floor
Outside the ponderous oaken door;
And then she murmurs—'It is not his;
Waiting's the weariest weariness.'
And Ring gets up and imprints a kiss
On his wife's submissive cheek, and says:
'Love me, my love, and, perchance, the days
Will come when I am with you no more,
And Frithjof shall have you as of yore.

I am old and shall not linger long,
And Frithjof and you are young and strong.'

For Ring the Ruler knoweth right well
What his wife's coy honour never would tell.
He knows that her heart will never be his ;
He knows that she offers her cheek to his kiss
As the kiss of a father not of a lover ;
He knows that the dream of her life was over
When he wedded her from her southern home :
He knows she would fainer rove and roam
Over the pathless and pitiless sea
Than all the paradises that be
In the wide wide world ; and it grieves his heart
That his longing and hers must live apart.
To him she is ever a loving child,
Or a gentle bird that once was wild
And fain would fly to its mate again.
She would die to save him a pang or pain,
But love him, ah ! no—not love as a wife,
Such love and longing fled from her life
At a wedding-feast three winters ago,
Leaving behind in a garden of woe
Remorses and recollections
For scutcheons and memorial stones.

Right well doth Ring the Ruler know all,
And Ring the Ruler knoweth withal

That never so much as in a thought
Has his sweet sad Ingebjorg wrong'd him
     aught.
Did.Frithjof come to his hall that night,
He would bid him welcome, to see the light
Dawn over Ingebjorg's face once more
As it did in the golden morns of yore.
Frithjof the Strong was an outcast man,
And twice had he outrag'd Baldur's fane,
And all held him accurst with one accord ;
But Frithjof had never broken his word
Or stoop'd to aught dishonest or mean.
He'd rather trust the accurst with his queen
Than Helgi the Ritual with a slave,—
For brave men love to honour the brave :
And what greater honour the wide world over
Than to trust a queen's honour to her lover ?
Right glad would he be did Frithjof abide
Here in his palace until he died,
So that he saw her smile as of yore,
And the gladness leap in her pulse once more.

He look'd at his queen ; the great grey eyes
Which bent on him in such simple wise
Were glancing nervously at the door.
She was list'ning—yes, up the sanded floor
Came a sturdy tread : does she know that tread ?
Why sighs she and droops her graceful head ?

A crooked old man in a ragged cloak
Begs shelter and food of the serving folk ;
The tallest among them chooses to jest
That any so mean and so meanly drest
Should venture into the hall of a king.
The stranger strides at him, threatening,
And, seizing his waist with either hand,
Tosses him heavily on the sand.
Ring the Ruler stepp'd down from his throne,
Saying, ' Stranger, that was bravely done ;
Nor do I think that your equipage
Accordeth with your prowess and age.
The fingers that lightly grasp'd and flung
Our serving-man were not old, but young :
Strip off your age and show us your youth.'
But Frithjof answer'd him, very loath,
' There is one in your hall who must not know
That I am here.'   ' Is it even so ? '
Quoth Ring.   ' I had thought you knew no fear ;
But since it is so, I, Ring, do swear
That none shall scathe a hair of your head.'
Then Frithjof, nursing a secret dread
That Ring would question him of his name,
And who were his fathers, and whence he came,
And trusting in Ingebjorg that she
Would never betray him wittingly,
Threw off his beggarly weeds, and stood
In the pride of his youth and manlihood.

Ingebjorg utter'd never a word,
But every little she saw or heard
Shed such a flushing over her face
As had not been there this three years' space :
Her wistful and wonderful grey eyes
Fed upon him in sweetest surprise.
She almost started up from her seat
And hardly might curb her impulse to greet
The beloved with salutation meet;
But when she remember'd where she was,
And the forethought of true love pleading its
     cause,
Sank on the stool by the throne again.
And Frithjof gazed upon her full again ;
And King the Ruler call'd to her, 'Sweet,
Give to the stranger a welcome meet
And kiss him upon his lordly mouth,
And fetch him a horn to quench his dreuth.'
And Ingebjorg kissed him all trembling ;
And neither spake or look'd at the king,
But their eyes made a wondrous questioning,
And answer'd before the question came :
Question and answer were one and the same.
Now all that evening sate the three
By the fire on the dais merrily,
And she, the still and sorrowful, smil'd
As she had been a generous child
By disappointment undefil'd.

Frithjof and Ingebjorg.

Soon Ring the Ruler closed his e'en,
And in a low voice bade his queen
Talk to the stranger while he slept;
But all that while a watch he kept
Under his lids ajar, and heard
Every sound and every word.
And there they sat till break of day,
But never a word of home spake they,
Or self, or hope, or fear, or youth, —
Only their eyes told the tender truth.
Ingebjorg asked of Thorsten's son
All he had dared and all he had done
In the years of his roving on the sea.
He told her of his voyages three
In the past three years, and once he told
Of the burning of Baldur's fane of gold;
And then both flush'd, and the hearty king
Smiled in his simulate slumbering.
But he thought, ' Right loyal is his tongue,
And truly this is Frithjof the Strong.
Never a word spake he all night long
That he might not have said to all I ween,
And loyal is Ingebjorg, the queen.
Great pity it is that they were not wed;
Of a truth their love is nowise dead,
But living and longing still to night;
Ingebjorg is as blithe and as bright

Frithjof and Ingebjorg.

As never she was this past three years.
Laughing and smiling, sobbing and tears,
Have been strange to her from then till now ;
She drank in life from those lips I trow
And shall drink of them again when I—
I am old and 'tis time that I should die.'
Then he opened his eyes and said, ' O Sir,
I have kept you long :' but the Berserker
Spake never a word, and the queen knelt down,
And, lifting her sweet eyes towards his own,
Look'd at him gratefully, and he knew
That her heart and honour were whole and true,
And kissed her fondly, and prayed soon to die
On the fair field of battle manfully.

IV.

Ring the Ruler would out to the chase
With Frithjof the valiant and the strong ;
They halted not for a moment's space
But follow'd the quarry all day long.
At length they came to a rugged place,
On three sides girt with precipice,
And on the fourth with a wide abyss.
Here Ring the Ruler lay down to sleep,
As in a slumber heavy and deep,
Leaning his head against Frithjof's knee,
As readily and as fearlessly

As tho' it had been upon his queen's.
And Frithjof, eyeing him as he leans,
Feels Angurvadel his magic sword :
As he thinks on his lost lov'd Ingebjorg,
It seem'd to wriggle out of its sheath,
And he saw the red runes underneath
Glowing a deeper and fiercer red,
And thoughts would arise, if one were dead,
Of dreams and dead darling hopes fulfil'd.
What matter were it if one were kill'd ?
But even ere the impulse was gone,
There pleaded a timid undertone,
' He is thy ally, thy friend, thy host,
And thou art a debtor to his trust.'
And then he sheath'd his sword again ;
And Ring would shudder as do men
O'ertaken by an evil dream.
But ever and again 'twould gleam
An inch or two beyond the sheath,
And ever and anon his death
Seem'd goodly to a hungry heart.
And then he ey'd the blade apart ;
And as the red runes redder grew,
Not knowing what the wish might do,
He hurl'd it into the abyss ;
And Ring the Ruler heard it whiz,
And, gazing at his uprais'd hand,
Said, ' Tell me, where is now thy brand ? '

And Frithjof answered him, 'O king,
Know that I did a goodly thing
In that it lies in the abyss ;
For to that Angurvadel is
A strange and magic power wed ;
For when the runic rhymes blaze red,
Whoever holdeth it doth feel
The Berserk madness o'er him steal,
And knoweth not to fear or spare,
But only how to do and dare ;
And Angurvadel bade me slay
An old man as asleep he lay,
That I might wed me with his queen :
You know not who I am, I ween.'
And King gave answer, 'Thou art he
The lord of ev'ry sound and sea ;
The strongest man of all the earth,
And glory of thy native North ;
Thou art that Frithjof whose great love
Set Ingebjorg the fair above
All other fair.   I knew thee when
Thou moved'st among the serving-men ;
I knew thee when thou drewed'st out,
Unaided, save by sinews stout,
My sled and horses from the bay,
When underneath the ice we lay ;
I knew thee by thy wind-swift feet,
For none on earth might be so fleet ;

I knew thee best of all to-day—
For who but thee would fling away
Thy sword to save another's life,
Who liv'd but for that other's wife?
But know that, tho' I bade you keep
And watch, and laid me down to sleep,
I did not sleep, but watched to see
The temper of your loyalty.
1 knew the struggle in your soul
'Twixt selfishness and self-control;
I heard the magic sword-blade gride
In fierce impatience at your side ;
I saw you glare upon the runes,
And felt the palpitations
Of heart and hand ; but still I lay
To prove if you would spare or slay,
For little cared I in my heart,
Since well I know I soon must part,
And fain would die a warrior's death
Rather than render up my breath
To weeping wife and serving crone.
So shall I win a fitting throne
In High Valhalla, where the brave
Rise not but thro' a soldier's grave.
But bide a little while, I pray,
Until my old life melts away,
As much I think it will ; and thou,
By Odin, sire of all, I vow,

Shalt wed with Ingebjorg the fair
And rule my people, for my heir
Is over young and weak to sway
The warrior Northmen, who obey
Those who can make their orders good,
And reverence nought but hardihood.'
And Frithjof answered him, ' O King,
Know that I may not do this thing,
For look I cannot on your queen
Without recalling what has been ;
And looked I often, I might be
Tempted to blot my loyalty,
For Ingebjorg is passing sweet,
And hearts will burn and pulses beat.
Ingebjorg hath simple eyes
Babbling of ancient sympathies,
And stray'd I near her golden head,
I might say what were best unsaid.'

Then Ring the Ruler answered him
With unbelieving glance and grim,
' Frithjof, if things be in this wise,
Why did you come in such a guise
To carry Ingebjorg away ? '
Then Frithjof answering did say,
' All-father knows I did not come
To steal thy lady from her home ;
I came, indeed, to this your shore

To look upon her face once more,
Thinking, when this one glimpse was o'er,
To live my life out on the main
And never look on her again.
For her alone I wore disguise,
To hide me from her loving eyes,
And not in fear of any man.
But when that wrestling bout began,
You bade me, if I did not fear,
In mine own proper guise appear ;
And I obey'd : and ever since
I hourly glance away, and wince
Under that loving, longing gaze,
Which bids me dream of other days,
And deem that one thing yet may be ;
Then, chiding my disloyalty,
I turn away from her to you.
Now know this that with honour due
I may not tarry ; but, O King,
I crave of you one little thing,
Never to let your lady know
The loving fears that bid me go,
Lest she should wail, or ail, or pine
For what may not be hers or mine.'

    Ring answer'd, ' Of a certainty,
O Frithjof, this may never be,
For know that, if you fall or fly,

The queen, sweet soul, will pine and die;
And though I now am waxing old,
My heart and blood are not so cold
As not to love her overmuch;
And seeing that my love is such,
I would not give that tender heart
A single pang or passing smart.
You have not over-long to wait;
Already do I see my Fate
With the remorseless scissors girt
Lurking behind to-morrow's skirt:
I pray you bide a little space.'
But Frithjof answer'd him apace,
'Alas! this may not be, O King.'
To whom the elder, answering,
'O Frithjof, bide with me to-night;
To-morrow thou shalt see a sight
Of import ominous and strange;
Whereat thy mind, maybe, will change.'
Then Frithjof answer'd, 'I obey;
Be it, my father, as you say.'
Once more the elder, 'I would fain
We three should sup to-night again
Together, as we supp'd before,
Ere thus we part for evermore.'
And once more Frithjof, 'I obey;
Be it, my father, as you say.'

v.

To-night your eyes are bright, sweetheart,
　　To-night's a truce to sorrow,
To-night—to-morrow we must part,
　　Must part for aye to-morrow.

You lov'd me years ago, you said,
　　As sister loves not brother ;
You lov'd me, but were forced to wed
　　Another—ah ! another.

I longed to see the light of yore.
　　I've seen it.　Oh ! and never
May I be lighten'd with it more ;
　　At noon we part for ever.

The day was dawning, still the three
Sat on the dais, outwardly
With cheerful faces ; but for one
Cruelly the hours sped on ;
For he has sworn to quit that shore,
This very noon, for evermore.
This noontide he must leave the queen,
Leave her with her gracious e'en
And silent wistful continence,
That wrong'd in nought the confidence

Imposed upon her by the king
In his simple cherishing.
'Twas small blame to her, if delight
Would make her glistening eyes more bright
When Frithjof told the feats he'd done,
Back'd by his Vikings or alone ;
Nor was she, as I think, to blame
If swiftly the red glory came
Into the fairness of her face
When Ring would dwell upon the grace
And glory of her early love :
But never o'er the brow above
Did frown or fleeting passion rove
For him she lov'd and would have wed ;
But sometimes to herself she said,
' Alas, and if it might have been.'
But outwardly with calm serene
She rais'd her fair face to the king
And strove to smile a welcoming :
Strong Frithjof on this last sweet night
Had scarcely strength to bear the sight.

Awhile did silence reign, then Ring
Said to his queen, ' I have a thing
To break to you, my pretty one—
Our mighty Frithjof sails to-noon.'
She did not speak, or shriek, or swoon,
But from the pinkness of her face
The blood and brightness fell apace :

She did not weep a tear ; her eyes
Were dry and daz'd with strong surprise
And glittered wildly, and her lips
Grew blanched and bloodless, and the tips
Of her white fingers nervously
Thrumm'd on her slack and shaking knee.

At last she strung her nerves and said,
' May not this sailing be delay'd?
His stay has been but short.'   But he
Answered the lady steadfastly,
Though scarce less faintly than she spake,
' It may not, and farewell I take
For ever of your kindly shore.'
The old king bade her press him more :
' More blandly can you plead, I trow,
And better than you pled but now.'
Then said the queen, ' O valiant sir,
I pray your courtesy to defer
Your sailing for a little space.'
He answered her, ' I pray your grace
And courtesy to let me part.'
But Ring the Ruler said, ' Sweetheart,
Your quiver is not arrowless ;
Ask him for your sake to do this.'
She said, ' Sweet sir, I have a wish—
Pardon if it be womanish—
That you should linger on a while.'
He answered without grace or guile,

'Lady, I dare not.' But Ring said,
'Sweet one, if you bid as I bade,
I do not think that he would go.'
She said, 'I dare no more, for know
That we were plighted lovers once,
And did I loose my passions,
I might say overmuch, I fear.'
'Speak on,' he answered. Then with clear
And passionate utterance, she said :
'The blame be on your own kind head :
O Frithjof, darling, do not fly,
For if you leave me I shall die.'
But Frithjof said, 'I dare not stay;
Your honour biddeth me away.'
'O Frithjof, tarry, I implore,
A little more—a little more.'
But Frithjof held his eyes away,
And muttered still, 'I dare not stay.'
And then she wept, whereat the king
Grasp'd his sharp sword, and, threatening,
Said, 'Frithjof, I bid thee tarry here.'
But Frithjof cried, 'I do not fear,
But Thor forbid that I should fight
With one whose hairs are worn and white;
But do thou slay me, an' ye will—
'Tis time this stormy heart were still.'
E'en while he spake the falchion bare
Leapt from its scabbard into air.

Yet not at Frithjof did it come,
But manfully was driven home
Into the stout breast of its lord;
Then, as the stream of life outpour'd,
He hail'd them : 'Sweetheart Ingebjorg,
And thou, strong Frithjof, come, I pray,
To hear a dying warrior's say :
And first clasp right hand in right hand.
My wife, my people, and my land,
O Frithjof, do I leave to thee,
And my son's boyhood : promise me
That thou wilt teach him to be strong.
Reign thou, for he is over-young
To lord it over hearts like these ;
And do thou, if ye twain so please,
Wed Ingebjorg, my true fair wife.
And——' But the ruddy stream of life
Upgurgling from an inward wound
Chok'd him : he sank upon the ground.
But she had mark'd him reeling o'er,
And threw her body down before,
And caught his head upon her breast,
And to his intent eyes express'd,
With speechful glance, her gratitude.
All round the shielded Northmen stood
Looking in sorrow at their Ring,
Who, of a sudden rallying,
Call'd for his helmet and his shield,
And said, 'I go to a fair field

Fought by Valhalla's chivalry.
'Twere shame if I were unready
To battle with the outland men.'
And then his head sank back again ;
And all stood death-still.   But she said,
Weeping sweet tears, ' He is not dead.'
And then he rais'd his head once more,
And shouted as through battle roar,
' Ye Valkyr-sisterhood, I come,
My exile over, to my home ;
Have ye a good steed at the stall
And gold-rimm'd skull-cap in the hall
Empty for me ?   I was a king,
And though I died not combating,
I did not die, as cowards die,
But by my good sword manfully.'
And thereupon he leapt upright,
And said, ' O outland hero, fight ;
To-morning one or both must fall,
To-night we drink within the hall ; '
And, shouting thus, he fell down dead.
And Ingebjorg of the fair head
Said nought, but fell a-sorrowing :
Then all the Northmen clamouring,
Shouted, ' O Frithjof, be thou king.'
But Frithjof, ' Not so ; be it known
I will but rule ye till this one

Come to the stoutness of a man ;
For it was goodly blood that ran
Through the great heart that low doth lie.'
And then he took the fair-hair'd boy,
And setting him upon his shield,
Lifted him, as the shouting peal'd,
Over their tall heads towering,
As all the Northmen lift a king.
And lo, the while he held him up,
The boy-king, without swerve or stoop,
Leapt from the full height of his arm
Down to the ground, nor hurt nor harm
Took from his leap : then clamouring
The Northmen shouted, ' Be thou king,
And Frithjof rule us till thou grow.'
And the fair boy said, ' Be it so,'
And clung to Frithjof's mighty hand.

Meanwhile the sweet queen of the land
Rose from the body of her lord ;
And Frithjof cried, 'O Ingebjorg,
Lead and I follow : these will bring
The body of the dear dead king.'
And she into the palace pass'd,
With her the boy, and at the last
Came Frithjof : and the twain did come
Into that chamber of the home

Where Ingebjorg was wont to sit.
A growing glowing sunset lit,
With a shimmer soft and red,
The gold perfection of her head :
Her fair face stood out very fair,
Her eyes were lovely with a tear,
Her sweet mouth trembling with a sob,
Her white breast swelling with a throb ;
And part in sorrow, part in hope,
Then suddenly the tears sprang up,
As Ingebjorg fell on his breast,
And he soft breathing 'loveliest,'
Rain'd down the kisses on her neck,
Then rais'd an unresisting cheek
And mouth'd the pilgrim tears away,
And drew her on his knee to play
With her sweet body tenderly.
Sunn'd in the fond warmth of his eye,
She kiss'd his lips : thus they two sat
Until the sun sank 'neath the flat
Low rim of ocean.   Then they rose,
And stepping stilly through the house,
Pass'd to the body of the king ;
And Ingebjorg fell sorrowing,
As for a father, through the night :
But, when the morrow's dawn was bright,
They set him on his own good ship,
And girt his sword upon his hip,

And laced his helmet on his head,
And his stout shield beside him laid,
And slew his charger by his side,
Nosing its master as it died,
And happing on a seaward gale,
Hoisted his grim red-dragon sail,
And lit a great fire in the hold
With pitch and pine torch manifold.
And she went sailing out to sea ;
And then the wind fell suddenly :
But ere her clinker'd planks of pine
Had burned down to the water line,
Sprang up a whirlwind in her track
And swept her swiftly o'er the back
Of the horizon. And all said,
' The gods do mourn that Ring is dead.'
But Ingebjorg cried out, ' Not so :
All-father sent the wind to show
That Ring was wanted in the fray
Waged in Valhalla-gard to-day.'
And all assented clamouring.
This was the end of Ruler Ring.

Much is there yet untold to tell
Of pain and pleasure that befell
Strong Frithjof in his after-life.
Fair Ingebjorg he had to wife ;

Helgi the black-hearted was slain ;
Merry Halfdan came again
With his lovely girlish face,
Craving pardoning and grace.
• Ill had he been forced to do
And strong Frithjof loved him too.
Baldur next, as it might seem,
Came to Frithjof in a dream,
Teaching him to rear again
Fitting and accepted fane ;
And the site he chose therefor
Was where Frithjof hurl'd of yore
Angurvadel in the abyss,
When Ring's head lay under his,
Feigning sleep.   Ellidè lay
At her moorings in the bay,
Like an old horse at his stall.
That that made the image fall
Clung to Ingebjorg's white wrist :
None might move it, did they list.
Much unsaid was there to say
At the opening of my lay :
Many songs were left unsung
As the story sped along.
These perchance some later day,
When I am not over-young,
And my lyre is better strung,
Will beguile an hour away.

THE SQUIRE'S BROTHER.

I.

You, sitting in your ancient hall
  Before a beech-log fire,
Think that the elder should have all :
  Of course you do—you're squire.
I, sitting on a three-rail fence
  Beneath a Queensland sun,
Think that the law shows little sense
  To give the younger none.
Nell wouldn't know me, I suppose,
  Were she to see me now,
Thus lolling in a linen blouse
  And bearded to the brow :
I didn't wear a flannel shirt
  When I was courting her,
Or buck-skin pants engrained with dirt
  And shiny as a spur.
I daresay that she pictures me
  In patent-leather boots,
A tall white hat (an I. and B)
  And one of Milton's suits :

That was the Charlie whom she knew
   Before the old man died ;
I wonder, would she take this view,
  , If she were by my side.

How beautiful she look'd that night !
   She seldom look'd so fair ;
And how the soft wax-candle light
   Show'd up her auburn hair !
She was a bit inclined to tease,
   To stand on P's and Q's,
To ' Keep your distance, if you please,'
   Until I told my news.
Then she rose up and took my hand,
   And look'd me in the face ;
And when in turn her face I scann'd
   I saw a tell-tale trace
Extending from the brave blue eyes
   Along the dimpled cheek,
The while she told in simple sighs
   The tale she would not speak.
She never let me kiss before,
   But now she gave her mouth
So frankly, that I almost swore
   I would forswear the South—
The sunny South of prospect vast—
   And hug the barren North,

E

Had she not bid me hold it fast,
    And, weeping, sent me forth.

So here I am—a pioneer,
    Working with my own hands
Harder than any labourer
    Upon my brother's lands,
Far from the haunts of gentlemen
    In this outlandish place ;
I wonder if I e'er again
    Shall see a woman's face.
I couldn't stand it, but for this,
    That, when I first came out,
I used to see the carriages
    In which men drove about,
Who'd tended sheep themselves of old
    'Neath Caledonia's rocks,
And now were lords of wealth untold,
    And half a hundred flocks.
I laid this unction to my heart,
    That, if a Scottish hind
Could play so manfully his part,
    I should not be behind :
And so I slave and stay and save,
    And squander nought but youth :
Nell sometimes writes and calls me brave,
    And knows but half the truth.

Do you suppose that old Sir Hugh,
    Who won your lands in mail,
Show'd half the valour that I do
    In sitting on this rail?
He tilted in his lordly way,
    And stoutly, I confess;
But I stand sentry all the day
    Against the wilderness.
There isn't much poetical
    About an old tweed suit,
And nothing chivalrous at all
    About a cowhide boot;
Yet oft beneath a bushman's breast
    There lurks a knightly soul,
And bushmen's feet have often press'd
    Towards a gallant goal.

So here I am, and, spite of hope,
    I hope in long years more
That I shall save sufficient up
    To seek my native shore.
And so I slave and stay and save,
    And squander nought but youth;
And if Nell said that I was brave
    She only told the truth.

II.

And is it true, or do I dream?
   Is this the dear old hall?
These the old pictures? Yes! I seem
   To recognise them all.
That is my father in his pink
   Upon his favourite hack,
I wonder what would Nellie think
   If she knew I were back?
That is my brother—he is changed,
   And heavier than he was
When years ago the park he ranged
   With me on ' Phiz' and ' Boz.'
His figure is a trifle full,
   His whiskers edg'd with grey ;
And yet at Oxford he could pull
   A good oar in his day.
The photo in that frame is Nell—
   Why, I gave Dick that frame ;
And doesn't the old pet look well?
   I swear she's just the same
As when I left her years ago
   To cross the southern foam.
I wonder if they've let her know
   That I'm expected home.

How well the artist coloured it ;
   He caught the sunny shades
That ever and anon would flit
   • Across her auburn braids.
But no !—that isn't quite the blue
   That shone in Nellie's eyes ;
Their light was nearer in its hue
   To our Australian skies.
White suits her best—she wore a white
   Of some soft silky weft
Upon that memorable night,
   The night before I left ;
Just such a graceful flowing train
   Then rippled as she moved ;
I'd like to see her once again,
   The lady that I loved.

I wonder what I'm staring at ;
   This is a real dress-coat ;
A veritable white cravat ·
   Is tied about my throat ;
I've had a dress-suit on before,
   And yet, I'm sure, I feel
Just like an awkward country boor
   Ask'd to a Sunday meal.
I can't bear sitting here alone,
   It seems so strange and sad,
Now that my father there is gone,
   And I'm no more a lad.

'Twas here he nursed me on his knee
  In that old high-back'd chair ;
I'd give ten thousand down to see
  The old man sitting there.

What was that footstep?—not old John's?
  His boots have such a creak ;
I'd almost swear I knew the tones,
  And heard a woman speak ;
The steps come nearer, and the door—
  What is it stirs my heart?
Why should a footstep on the floor
  Cause every nerve to start?
A lady scanning with her eye
  A letter in her hand,
Bending her way unconsciously
  Almost to where I stand.
I think I know that writing well :
  Of course—why it's my own,
And she who reads it thus is Nell.—
  Together and alone !

III.

A lady in her bedroom stands
  Before a faded carte,
Wistfully folding her white hands,
  Her sweet lips just apart.

Yes, he is back, she said at last,
   I thought he'd never come ;
Yet now when all these years are past
   •Since first he left his home,
It seems as if 'twas yesterday
   On which I bid him go.
He never would have gone away
   Had I not forced him to ;
And yet eleven years have flown :—
   I did not hear him come,
And went to read his note alone
   In the big dining-room.
I don't know if I laughed or cried,
   My eyes were full of tears,
To find my lover by my side
   After the lonely years.
He took my hands, we did not speak
   For full a minute's space ;
I don't know who was first to break
   The silence of the place.
Charlie is alter'd : he was once
   Blasé—and little more—
Who thought it fine to be a dunce,
   And everything a bore ;
Who wore the closest-fitting coats
   Of any in 'The Row,'
And patent-leather button'd boots—
   A kind of Bond-Street beau ;

Yet capable of better things
 When out of Fashion's swim,
Or I, who scorn mere tailorlings,
 Should not have borne with him.
But Charlie's heart was of good stuff,
 And of the proper grit ;
Men always found it true enough
 When they had tested it.
He is much alter'd ;—when I saw
 His dignified dark face,
I knew that changes had come o'er
 His life in that wild place.
I read the story in his eyes,
 I heard it in his voice,
The glad news that she ought to prize,
 The lady of his choice.
He must be more than dull of soul
 Who in the open West
Sees leagues on leagues of prairie roll,
 And is not soul-impress'd ;
Who knows that he may hold for his
 As far as he can see
Into the untamed wilderness
 From top of highest tree ;
Who feels that he is all alone,
 Without a white man near
To share or to dispute his crown
 O'er forest, plain, and mere ;

The Squire's Brother.

With nought but Nature to behold,
  No confidant but her :
He must be of the baser mould
 • Or feel his spirit stir.

I'd rather marry him than Dick,
  Though Dick is an ' M.P.'
Lord of the manor of High Wick,
  A 'D.L.' and 'P.C.'
' Right Hon.' before your name, I know,
  Is coveted by all,
And one needs courage to forego
  A gabled Tudor hall.
I always wish Dick would not seem
  So like a well-fed dog,
And on his life's unruffled stream
  Float so much like a log ;
The world has been so good to him
  That he has never known
How hard it sometimes is to swim
  For some poor shipwreck'd one.
But Charlie's very different,
  He's seen the real world,
And where no white man ever went
  His lonely flag unfurl'd ;
He went to slave and stay and save,
  And squander'd nought but youth ;
And when I said that he was brave
  I knew but half the truth ;

For there in intermittent strife,
  With hostile natives waged,
He spent the best years of his life
  In hum-drum toil engaged ;
Or galloping the livelong day,
  Under a Queensland sun,
After some bullocks gone astray
  Or stolen off the run.
He's handsomer, I think, to-day,
  Although he is so brown,
And though his hair is ting'd with grey,
  And thin upon the crown,
Than in the days when he was known
  At ' White's ' as Cupid Forte,
And in good looks could hold his own
  With any man at Court.

Well he has come and ask'd again
  That which he came to ask
The night before he crossed the main
  Upon his uphill task.
I answer'd as I answer'd then,
  But with a lighter heart.
Who knew if we should meet again
  The day we had to part ?

IV.

'Neath a verandah in Toorak
　I sit this summer-morn,
While from the garden at the back,
　Upon the breezes borne,
There floats a subtle, faint perfume
　Of oleander bow'rs,
And broad magnolias in bloom,
　And opening orange flow'rs.

A lady 'mid the flow'rs I see,
　Moving with footsteps light,
And when she stoops she shows to me
　A slipper slim and bright,
An ankle stocking'd in black silk
　And rounded as a palm,
Her dress is of the hue of milk,
　And making of Madame.
I wonder is that garden-hat
　Intended to conceal
All but that heavy auburn plait,
　Or merely to reveal
Enough to make one long to catch
　A glimpse of what is there,
To see if eye and feature match
　The glory of the hair?

That is my Nellie—she's out here
    As Mrs. Cupid Forte :
We came to Melbourne late last year ;
    I could not bear the thought
Of snow, and sleet, and slush, and rain,
    And yellow London fogs :
An English winter, I maintain,
    Is only fit for frogs.
The night when first again we met—
    Alone, by some good-luck—
I ask'd if she'd repented yet
    The bargain we had struck ?
She answer'd that she was too old,
    That what few charms she'd had
Had faded in the years that roll'd
    Since we were girl and lad.
And all the while she was as fair
    As ever she had been ;
Years had not triumph'd to impair
    The beauties of eighteen.
The same slight figure as of yore,
    The same elastic gait,
As she had had ten years before,
    Were hers at twenty-eight ;
And had her girlish loveliness
    Lost aught of its old grace,
And had there been one shade the less
    Of *esprit* in her face,

I had no calling to upbraid,
  And tell the bitter truth,
For whom she let her beauty fade
  And sacrificed her youth.
Look at her as she stoops to pull
  That rosebud off its briar,
Do you not think her beautiful
  As lover could desire?
Heard you that laughter light and sweet,
  That little snatch of song?
Do they sound like the counterfeit
  Of one no longer young?

Here 'neath the clear Australian sky
  I lead the life of kings,
'Mid everything that tempts the eye,
  Or soothes the sufferings ;
Wealth, and a woman kind and fair,
  Fine horses and fine trees,
Children, choice fruits, and flowers rare,
  And health, and hope, and ease.

SAPPHO.

(A DREAM.)

I.

THE full moon glitters on the sand,
The North Sea ripples on the strand,
The low cliff's shadow from above
Falls on a little landlock'd cove,
Which, deep and dang'rous to the edge,
Mines underneath the chalky ledge,
Save where the bank, with gentle sink,
Slopes downward to the water's brink.
Here Harold stood : the night was clear,
And through the purple atmosphere
The stars ~none brightly, and the sea
Sang chorus to his rhapsody :
A man whom all might happy deem,
And women love, and men esteem ;
Full broad of shoulder, strong of arm,
And deaf to anger or alarm,
But chivalrous in hastiness
To champion trouble or distress ;

As great in spirit as in frame,
In danger and distress the same,
With wild, dark, handsome, haunting face—
And strength in manhood serves for grace :
Able was he to hold his own,
And worthy admiration ;
Accustom'd since he scarce could stand
To the stern pastimes of his land :
At first to shoulder off the stool
The other little boys at school,
And then to wrestle and to fight
With ten-year rivals, his delight ;
Then competition took the place
Of stand-up fighting face to face ;
There were brave battles to be fought
In beating other boys at sport ;
And as the rolling years went on
Great glory in such sports he won ;
Fours to true leg, straight spanking drives
Snick'd twos and threes, clean cuts for fives,
Fast ripping balls, well on the wicket,
Made him renown'd in Rugby cricket.
Hot ' hacks ' exchanged, 'tries ' dearly bought ;
A hero in the sterner sport.
He'd stalk'd the red deer over Highland rocks ;
He'd ' taken ' untried fences for the fox ;
In Kentish copses, 'neath an autumn sun,
The largest bag had fallen to his gun ;

In Norway rivers, waist-deep in the flood,
Salmon of weight had yielded to his rod ;
Alone, afoot, on many a weary day,
O'er steep wet moor and featureless highway,
He strode to fields of unforgotten fights
Of Rupert's cavaliers and Clifford's knights ;
To storied castles shatter'd in the war
'Twixt Crown and Commons, minsters where of yore
Dunstan and Baeda fed the sacred light
Of learning in the long dark English night ;
To abbeys rich with knightly founders' bones,
And gifts of bygone heroes and kings' sons :
To great cathedrals hallow'd by the pray'r
Of great dead men ; to cities famed and fair ;
To torrents foaming, fretting, falling fast,
And mighty rivers slowly sailing past
By stately halls and immemorial trees ;
To lonely wolds and humming village leas,
Green downs, and grey gaunt mountains, and broad
  plains
Strewn with old chieftains' tombs and fallen fanes ;
To silent reed-fring'd lake and lone sea-shore,
As silent, save for surf and storm wind's roar.
He knew the names of all the stars in heaven—
The heralds of the morning and the even ;
He knew the names of all the birds that fly,
And beasts that range beneath the Northern sky,
And many fish that in the north seas ply ;

He knew the gauzy denizens of air,
And had a hoard wherein the rich and rare
Of daily butterfly and nightly moth
Were ranged together, and he knew in troth
The name of every flow'r that wood and field
From Cornwall to Northumberland do yield.

Ballads he knew, and many a legend old
In knightly Kent and daring Devon told,
And many a border-boast and roundelay
Sung in the good green wood : these he would say
Word by word, line by line, and verse by verse,
After the croonings of a fond old nurse,
Who had nought else to teach him : these he knew,
And sought out many other when he grew,
In dingy quarto bought at fusty stall
Or 'neath old cottage prints fantastical.
Oft far into the night he converse held
With the great minds and noble hearts of eld—
Caedmon and Mallory, and old Geoffry,
The sire and sieur of English poesy ;
Spenser and More and Shakspere, England's voice,
In whom the ears of ages shall rejoice ;
Sweet Sidney, Beaumont, Fletcher, 'rare old Ben,'
And glorious Milton, brave John Bunyan,
Pepys, Evelyn, Clarendon, Addison,
Dick Steele, Defoe and Swift—these he would con,

F

And Keats and fairy Shelley, who could tell
The sadness of all happiness too well ;
And Landor, he to whom 'twas given to show
The longings and the life of long ago.
    And often to these meetings at midnight
Came old school friends he'd studied with delight,
Not diligence : Homer the editor,
And Hesiod the old, and many more ;
Dear babbling, loosely-learn'd Herodotus,
Euripides, Sophocles, Æschylus,
Plato and Aristotle ; and the soft
Anacreon came with them ; nor less oft
Came sage Lucretius and Cicero,
Virgil and witty Horace, Gallio
And legendary Livy ; oft too came
The second sire of poetry--a flame
From his own Hell was burning in that breast,
Whence the triunal vision was express'd—
Condemn'd, his love unknown and dead, to roam
In poor and painful exile from his home.
And with him came Messer Boccaccio,
Full of the loves and jests of long ago ;
And many a bard who'd listed to his tales,
And sung them o'er again, and one from Wales,
And one from Alcalà, and many more
Whose names were writ in fire, in days of yore.

    And sometimes, when he heard the stirring hum
Of music or great shoutings, there would come

Heroes and hosts : Herman and Hannibal,
Etzel, the Cid, Roland of Roncesvalles,
Harold of Hastings, Richard Lion-heart
And Edward the Black Prince ; nor far apart,
Hawkins and Drake, Raleigh and Frobisher,
And the great Howard, Ironside Oliver
And his Ironsides, and Rupert, hand-on-sword,
And Buonaparte, and he who cross'd the ford
Against advice and conquer'd on that day
When he won Plassey and England India :
And those Six Hundred heroes.   And at times,
Releas'd by midnight's necromantic chimes,
Came the true lovers and wild souls of yore—
Dauntless Medea, one from Naxos' shore,
Helen and light-heart Paris, Psyche true,
Aspasia and the masterman who drew
More glory from her sweetness than the sway
Of Athens in her hour, and Thaïs gay,
Who ruled the world's commander : with these came
Dido and lone Iarbas, hearts of fame,
That lov'd at odds ; and some of later name—
Abelard, Heloïse, and Rosamond,
And Castile's Eleanor, whose love was found
Proof against poison, and the Florentine
Who bore deep graven on his heart divine
The little maid twice seen through years of power
And years of pain ; and many a rare hour

F 2

Came the white Queen of Scots.   Here all who fell
Victims to service true, or lov'd too well,
Were welcome, for his wild heart long'd to know
Such love as beauty tender'd long ago.

      Indeed, he ev'ry gift could boast
But the three gifts he valued most—
Wealth to pet beauty, beauty's self,
Won for his own sake, not for pelf,
And laurels of a poet : he
Enough had tasted of all three
To thirst for more.   To many a maid
His fancy 'd for a moment stray'd ;
Blue eyes and hazel, grey and brown,
Had answer'd frankly to his own ;
Auburn and flaxen, black and gold,
Had mesh'd his heart in glossy fold ;
But ever came an undertone
Of something wanting in each one.
The lady of his choice should be
Sublime in her simplicity,
Of lowly mind and high estate,
And fairy-light in grace and gait ;
One who would try to understand
Whate'er he wrote, whate'er he plann'd ;
With fitful anger for defence
Against abus'd obedience,

And just sufficient patience
To obviate unjust offence ;
With beauty intellectual,
The rarest witchery of all,
And curly clustering wealth of hair
Indented by a forehead fair,
And broad and creamy ; thoughtful eyes,
Open in innocent surprise,
Melting in pity, fired in wrath,
Pouring the soul's whole secret forth
In love, not unacquaint with tears.
She must have tender girlish fears,
And a soft voice, with elfin mirth,
And presence equal to her birth ;
She must be coy—the more they cost
More dear they are, the dearest most ;
But when she yields let her confess
With all the gentler tenderness,
And hungry kiss and hot caress.
Passion and love walk hand in hand :
Content is imitation bland
For widowers and second wives,
And men whose ledgers are their lives ;
Youth's passion-flow'r is delicate
And, blighted, blossoms not till late.

Sooth'd by the sweet salt soughing breeze,
He linger'd over shapes like these :

Now peering from the ledge above
Into the clear depth of the cove;
Now gazing upward at a star,
And now across the sea afar,
To a lithe schooner-yacht that lay,
Nodding her slim masts, on the bay;
When suddenly he heard the plash,
And saw the phosphorescent flash
Of dipping oars, and then a skiff,
Making the shore beneath the cliff.
A muffled lady and old man
Sat in the stern-sheets; soon it ran
To where the coast with gradual sink
Sloped downwards to the water's brink.
   The old man rose, and lightly sprung
Ashore, and safe. The shallop swung
Just as his daughter leapt, and she
Sank in the clear depth of the sea;
She swerv'd and sank without a sound,
And as she fell the scarf unwound
That veil'd her features, and laid bare
A sweet fair face and gold of hair
Crowning it; as she sank she smiled,
And shot a glance intense and wild
Up at the ledge where Harold stood.
He in a strange ecstatic mood
Was gazing downwards at the flood,

And the wet face, which seem'd to be
That of a goddess of the sea ;
Then in he plung'd : she gripp'd his arms
And, in the terror that disarms
The mind of reason, dragg'd him down,
As Sirens in the legend drown
   The victims of their song.
He thought in that short minute's space
Of his long start and ill-run race,
   Of all the waste and wrong
That crowded in his misspent life,
Of all the soarings and the strife
   Of his foreshorten'd day,
Of ev'ry uncompleted aim,
Of unachiev'd desire of fame,
   And chances slipp'd away :
And ere his senses lost control
He thought of his immortal soul,
   And felt he could not pray.

   *   *   *   *

THE DREAM.

He, standing by the landlock'd cove,
Built airy palaces of love,
And, leaning over, strove to peer
Beneath the starlit waters clear,

When suddenly arose a maid
Out of the depth, and, unafraid,
Swam near him, and in sweet, soft voice
Bade Harold welcome, and rejoice.
' At last,' she said, ' my love, thou'rt come :
Thou hast been long away from home.'
He look'd at her, but could not tell
What maid it was that lov'd him well,
And said, ' Who are you, sweet ? ' but she—
' Wilt thou renew thy cruelty,
Erst cruel Phaon ? know'st thou not
Thy bride, thy Sappho ? From my grot
Beneath the ocean oft have I
Gazed upward at the shore and sky
To see thee once again ; and now
Thou'rt come. I pray thee, dear heart, vow
That thou wilt ne'er forsake me more
For idle dalliance on the shore,
But seek in love's unfailing arms
A shelter from the world's alarms,
And pillow'd on a white warm breast
Lull thine o'er-labour'd head to rest.'

He edg'd a step toward the cove,
Irresolute 'twixt life and love;
She swam a stroke toward the shore,
Pleading and beckoning the more,
And said, ' I loved those wilful curls
As none among the Lesbian girls :

No maid in Mitylene 'd prize
Gems, as I prized those glad brown eyes—
I, who the love of man defied,
Offered my beauty to your pride,
And you despised it ; then I wail'd,
And all my joy in living fail'd,
And oft I sought a lonely rock
That quiver'd with the billows' shock,
And bore my burthen to the breeze,
And sang my sorrows to the seas ;
And last I plung'd, in hope to be
Reprieved by death from misery.

' But the mermen pined for the love of me,
    As I sang to the sea and sky;
And those who are loved by kings of the sea
    May be drown'd, but cannot die.

' Their kisses I loath'd, and I loath'd their love,
    The more as they prov'd more true ;
And all the day long I would rove and rove,
    Watching and waiting for you.

' Then lay down your weary head in my arms,
    And you shall a merman be,
And reign as a king in the careless calms
    Of the fathomless sapphire sea.'

Harold.

'But I have joys I cannot leave:
  The glory of morning and of eve,
    The glory of the noon ;
  The golden sun that shines on high,
  The stars embroider'd on the sky,
    The silver of the moon.'

Sappho.

'But the sun shines through the breast of the blue,
  And moon-finger'd waves are fair,
And the stars we view reflected anew
  On the gold of mermaid hair.'

Harold.

'But I have other joys than these :
  The cliffs and mountains, and the breeze
    That freshens round their tops ;
  The valleys with their kirtles green,
  The uplands with their shoulders sheen
    And coronal of copse.'

Sappho.

'There are hills and valleys below the deep
  Far fairer than any of earth ;
And the winds of your mountains wake and sleep,
  In the ocean that gives them birth.'

Sappho.

Harold.

‘ But I have fairy flow'rs that rise
. Fresh from their winter obsequies
  To decorate the spring ;
And others of a later day
To grace the summer, and delay
  The autumn's taking wing.’

Sappho.

‘ The sea-flowers are more glorious far,
  And they never sleep or die ;
Our anemones wear the shape of a star,
  And hue of a sunset sky.’

Harold.

‘ And I have groves whose living shade
  Is canopy and colonnade
    Beneath an August sun ;
Choice garden trees with fruitage fine,
And evergreens that never pine
    When August days are done.’

Sappho.

And under the sea there are gardens sweet,
  And coral groves red and white ;
We know not the changes of cold and heat,
  But love the sun for his light.’

Harold.

'The birds I love so fleet and fair
That glitter through the sunny air,
    And warble in the dawn ;
The insect-radiance of May,
Whose dotage closes with the day
    That saw their brightness born.'

Sappho.

'We have beautiful shapes and tuneful shells
In our wondrous world below ;
But the glories of ocean no one tells,
And none but the mermen know.'

Harold.

'But most of all I love to stand
On each grey castle of our land,
    And nodding Norman keep,
Telling with shatter'd walls and scars
A rugged tale of great old wars
    And warriors long asleep :
To muse on moss-hid arch and aisle
Of desecrate Cistercian pile
    And fane of long ago ;
To wander through a village street
Trod by a great man's childish feet
    While yet his lot was low ;

To gaze across a moor whereon
A famous victory was won
   Or some stout hero fell ;
And often have I fondly roved
Where two wild lovers met and lov'd,
   Not wisely, but too well.'

Sappho.

' We have no castles in ruin revered,
   No abbeys of long ago,
No villages where great men were rear'd
   While yet their lot was low.
But we have some rare old battle-grounds
   Where heroes were kill'd at bay,
And buried chiefs without burial mounds,
   And trystings of lovers gay.
Then lay down your wearied head in my arms,
   And you shall a merman be,
And reign as a king in the careless calms
   Of the fathomless sapphire sea.'

Harold.

' But under the sea, love, under the sea,
   What do you do for the clear blue sky ? '

Sappho.

' O ! the clear blue sea is a sky to me,
   And our heaven is not too high.'

Then in he plung'd : she drew him down,
As sirens in the legend drown
   The victims of their melody.
The waters gurgled in his ears,
   He deem'd that he must die ;
But Sappho sooth'd away his fears
   With kisses wooingly.
Down, down they sank until they reach'd
A sapphire-vaulted cavern beach'd
With jet and shells of pearl ; the walls
Were cataracts and waterfalls.
Here they abode full lovingly,
And smoothly the quick days sped by.
Sometimes he sits upon the rocks,
Upgathering her elfin locks ;
Sometimes she sits upon his knee,
 And sings him anthems of the sea ;
Sometimes upon the sand he lies,
Gazing at sea-blue steadfast eyes
   That concentrate on him ;
And sometimes for an hour's space
He dallies with a fair, fond face
   And body rounded slim.
She tells him legends of the deep,
And shows him where the mermen keep
   Their fleet of founder'd ships,
And where their milliard army lies
Of skeletons with hollow eyes
   And grinning jaws for lips.

But most of all she's used to tell
Of those old hours she lov'd so well,
   The hours of Lesbian song ;
To call back some sad roundelay,
That wiled away an elderday
   Whereon he linger'd long ;
To call back how it sooth'd to rove,
And tell the breezes of her love
   And waters of her woes ;
To whisper consummated bliss,
And seal her whisper with a kiss,
   And sink in sweet repose.

Thus sped they many a joyous day
In amorous and peaceful play,
Glad of a respite from the fears
Of eager and ambitious years.
But last it fell that Sappho's cheek
Grew hollow and her body weak :
He saw and griev'd until she broke
The silence, and the dull truth spoke :
   'We have no souls, dear love,
For had we souls we could not live
Without the elements that give
   The life they live above—
The daily drink, the daily fare
The sweet and all-sustaining air.'

' What matter' he cried, 'though we have no soul
    We shall live as long as the earth,
Without the millstone of care and control
    Which hangs round the neck from birth.

' We have all the wonders of deep and bay,
    And the heaven is ours above,
As much as the mortals who toil all day
    And have only the night for love.

' And if no future in heaven be ours
    When the earth is ended, we've this—
We can make a heaven of earthly hours,
    And sweeten our end with a kiss.'

Sappho.

' Though love is good and gracious ease,
Life is for nobler ends than these :
To build impregnably a name
And force unwilling grants from fame ;
To gain great victories, and give
A wise example how to live ;
To give your country liberty,
Or teach her patriots how to die ;
To chronicle your finest thought
For generations to be taught ;

With practice and with preaching win
A sinful people from their sin,
To point your tale and wing your song
As arrows against wrath and wrong.'

Though he for love and ease was fain,
His nobler nature woke again :
'Teach me, my love,' he said, 'once more
To win the souls we had before,
What toils attain, what pains restore.'

'It is writ in the Book of the Sea,' she saith,
   'That a merman a soul may gain
Who snatches the life of a man from death
   Or a maiden's love can attain.'
Then to the landlock'd cove they swam,
And when they to the inlet came
He saw a drowning maiden sink
In the clear depth beside the brink.
He seem'd to clasp her, as before,
And bear her breathing to the shore,
And, lo ! the maid in his embrace
Wore Sappho's form and Sappho's face.

The End of the Dream.

He woke : beside his pillow stood
More perfect in her womanhood
   The lady of his vision,
Her lips half parted for a smile
   In sweetest indecision,
Whether to fly or bide the while
   He ask'd of his position.
She stay'd : it needs no Chaldee seer
Or Arabic astrologer
   To guess their conversation ;
The meaning of the mystery
   Needs no interpretation ;
We leave the after-history
   To your imagination.

◄

FROM 'TROY.'

THE NIGHT BEFORE THE FALL.

The night had come, such night had never been
So sweetly soft, so gloriously serene.
After the glow and glory of the day,
After the clash and clamour of the fray,
Came a still night, the very winds at rest,
And spread a shroud o'er earth's poor mangled breast
The moon with trebly-bright effulgence falls
On fated Ilium's grim old god-built walls :

Is it a dream? or is the silver queen
Fixing a last fond gaze upon the scene?
The stars shine out their brightest through the sky,
Do they too feel that thou must die?
    Thus peaceful nature, not so peaceful man :
The voice of mirth throughout the city ran ;
From ev'ry portal stream, with shouts of joy,
Maids ten-years-pent within the walls of Troy ;
Their armour doff'd, the amorous Phrygian boys
Pursue the Phrygian maids with gladsome noise ;

The bards triumphant boast the fall of Greece
And chaunt their thanks for victory and peace ;
The laurell'd fanes resound with priestly tread,
While to the Gods the victims vowed they lead ;
The exultant roar of Troy gone up to heaven
Jars with the harmony of that sweet even.
Blind hearts ! your hour is brief as it is bright :
Sing sweet, wild swans of Troy, ye die to-night.
     So sported on the crowd in licence glad.
But one amid the general joy was sad :
Eëtion's daughter in the star-lit gloom,
Refusing comfort, moan'd her Hector's doom :
The tears, that tired not flowing, dimm'd the blue
Of those sweet eyes, which Hector knew so true ;

Prone on the rushen floor in sorrow fell
The golden head that Hector loved so well ;
The fair fond face, that thrilled him with its trust,
Was pale with sorrow, stained with tears and dust ;
Troy's sweetest woman, and the world's best wife
O'er her dead lord was weeping out her life.

A CHRISTMAS LETTER.

'Tis Christmas, and the North wind blows ;
   'Twas two years yesterday
Since from the Lusitania's bows
   I look'd o'er Table Bay,
 A tripper round the narrow world,
   A pilgrim of the main,
Expecting when her sails unfurl'd
   To start for home again.
And, steaming thence three weeks or more,
   I reach'd Victoria,
Upon her hospitable shore
   To make a few months' stay ;
But month on month unnoticed fled,
   And ere the year had come,
I chose the land I visited
   To be my future home.
'Tis Christmas, and the North wind blows ;
   Our hearts are one to-day,
Though you are mid the English snows
   I in Australia ;

You, when you hear the Northern blast,
 Pile coal upon your fires ;
We strip until the storm is past
 While every pore perspires.
I fancy I can picture you
 Upon this Christmas night,
Just sitting as you used to do,
 The laughter at its height :
And then a sudden, silent pause
 Coming upon your glee,
And kind eyes glistening because
 You chanc'd to think of me.
This morning when I woke and knew
 Christmas had come again,
I almost fancied I could view
 Rime on the window-pane ;
And hear the ringing of the wheels
 Upon the frosty ground,
And see the drip that downward steals
 In icy fetters bound.
I daresay you've been on the lake,
 Or sliding on the snow,
And breathing on your hands to make
 The circulation flow,
Nestling your nose among the furs
 Of which your boa's made ;
The Fahrenheit here registers
 A hundred in the shade.

It doesn't seem like Christmas here
 . With this unclouded sky,
This pure transparent atmosphere
    And with the sun so high ;
To see the rose upon the bush,
    The leaves upon the trees,
To hear the forest's summer hush
    Or the low hum of bees.

But cold winds bring not Christmastide,
    Or budding roses June,
And when it's night upon your side
    We're basking in the noon.
Kind hearts make Christmas—June can bring
    Blue sky or clouds above ;
The only universal spring
    Is that which comes with love.

And so it's Christmas in the South
    As on the North-Sea coasts,
Though we are starv'd with summer-drouth,
    And you with winter frosts.
And we shall have our roast beef here,
    And think of you the while,
Who in the other hemisphere
    Cling to the mother isle.
Feel sure that we shall drink to you,
    We who have wander'd forth ;

And many a million thoughts will go
　　To-day from South to North.
Old heads will muse on churches old
　　Where bells will ring to-day—
The very bells, perchance, which toll'd
　　Their fathers to the clay.
And now, good night ! maybe I'll dream
　　That I am with you all,
Watching the ruddy embers gleam
　　Over the panell'd hall :
Nor care I if I dream or not,
　　Though sever'd by the foam,
My heart is always in the spot
　　Which was my childhood's home.

WILTSHIRE.

I have been out in the forest to-day
    Plucking wild strawberry fruits,
I have watched the merry dormice at play
    By their holes in oaktree roots ;
I have chased the squirrel at dawn and dusk,
    And mark'd where the primrose grew,
While I trampled the empty acorn-husk
    And gather'd germanders blue.

I have wander'd over the downs to-day
    In the fragrant morning hours,
I was tracking the bee from spray to spray,
    As it rifled honey flow'rs ;
I heard all the song of the early lark
    From a cloud above me shed,
And I saw the daisy shut from the dark,
    The halo around her head.

I have been out in the city to-day,
  And have seen the merry sun,
I watch'd the city children at play
  When morning school was done ;
They could not go into the budding wood,
  Or paths by the corn-fields take,
To see the Bugle unfolding his hood
  And the Pimpernel awake.

They'd little wan faces and weary feet,
  And their very games were sad,
Outside the school-door in the dusty street—
  The only playground they had.
A public-house next to the corner stood—
  Perhaps their mothers were there—
And a funeral pass'd ; could they be good,
  Such sights and sounds in the air ?

' Pretty ones, why aren't you out in the lanes ? '
  I ask'd of two little girls
With faces like those on church window-panes
  And heads all cover'd with curls.
' There are roses climbing over the hedge,
  And tansies trailing below,
And blue forget-me-nots twined in the sedge ;
  You can watch the water flow.'

But when they summon'd up courage to speak,
  'We hate the country,' they said,
'Father used to get ten shillings a week,
  And now gets thirty instead ;
He used to come back in the ev'ning late
  And go off so very soon,
And now his work doesn't begin till eight,
  And stops in the afternoon.

'We hate the country,' the little ones said,
  'The circus never comes round,
And you can't buy jumbles or gingerbread,
  And sugar's so dear a pound :
We couldn't have half the ribbons and ties,
  And we had no parasol,
And we went to the church on Sunday twice
  As well as the Sunday school.'

I gave them some pennies to spend on buns,
  And walk'd up the street quite fast,
Wrapp'd up in my own meditations
  And heeding nothing I pass'd :
I thought to myself there was something wrong
  When children could talk like this,
And hate the green fields they were born among
  And think a factory bliss.

There's nothing to weary the eye in trees,
   And turf doesn't tire the feet,
One doesn't feel choked by the country breeze,
   And hedges, are they not sweet?
I liked the new milk when I was a boy,
   And loved blackberrying days,
And mightn't the children take some small joy
   In making wild-flow'r bouquets?

The hedges are surely the place for buds,
   The meadows for open flow'rs,
Little birds should sing away in the woods
   In the merry morning hours :
Little children should grow, as the young trees grow,
   Under the sun and the sky,
And their songs should go up as birds' songs go
   That hover and sing on high.

But you cannot expect a man to speak
   In the true poetic way
Of spots where he gets ten shillings a week
   And works twelve hours a day.
The master has something to answer for
   Who makes the country a curse,
And teaches the labourer to abhor
   The beautiful universe.

I suppose it came of the primal sin
    That profit should go with pain,
That wealth should be made in the smoke and din,
    And death dog the steps of gain.
For to have the loaf without the leaven,
    And the rose without the thorn,
Was never, I think, vouchsafed by heaven
    To a man of woman born.

THE TWO ROSES

I.

A dainty rose in a hothouse grew,
  Shelter'd from rain and stinted of dew,
Its fragrance was wafted the whole house through ;
  A delicate shape, a delicate hue,
  Yet only the great its sweetness knew.

II.

A wild dog-rose in a wild wood grew,
  Forced by the rain and fed by the dew,
Its fragrance was wafted the wide wood through ;
  A delicate shape, a delicate hue,
  And all the hamlet its sweetness knew.

III.

The hothouse flow'r had a courtly grace,
  And its leaves were trimm'd in courtly ways,
And its head rose fair in its fair high place ;
  But it ail'd and paled in the noontide blaze,
  And shrunk from the summer sun's full rays.

IV.

The wild dog-rose had its own wild grace,
And its leaves ran riot in wilder ways,
And its head hung sweet in its own sweet place ;
And it did not ail or pale in the blaze,
But lov'd the summer sun and his rays.

V.

The hothouse rose lived its little day,
Tenderly tended with culture and care,
Then waned and wasted and wither'd away,
Till all that was left of its dainties fair
Were a few brown petals hanging there.

VI.

The wild dog-rose lived its little day,
Unchecked by culture unaided by care,
Then faded and flutter'd and floated away ;
But instead of its petals hanging there
A hip grew rosy and ripe and fair.

VII.

The hothouse rose to the great was dear ;
Full many a lord had loved it, I ween,
For its lady's cheek was dainty and clear
As ever the rose's itself had been,
As fragrant, as fair, and as seldom seen.

VIII.

The wild dog-rose to the poor was dear ;
Full many a swain had fancied, I ween,
That his sweetheart's lips were dainty and clear
As ever the wild dog-rose's had been :
For fragrant and fair had he seldom seen.

IX.

The hothouse rose when shrunken and sere
Had petals as sweetly fragrant as e'er,
And a great lord made his bosom their bier,
Not that he heeded their fragrance rare,
But, rather, because his lady was fair.

X.

Out of the dog-rose shrunken and sere
Grew a hip as red as the rose was e'er ;
A nightingale, making her bosom its bier,
Sang sweetly—not because it was rare,
But rather, I think, that her voice was fair.

XI.

The hothouse rose, though shrunken and sere,
Was tended more tenderly now than e'er ;
Its mistress its lord had acknowledg'd dear,
And both of them thought its fragrance rare
Just because they were themselves so fair.

XII.

The wild dog-rose, though shrunken and sere,
    • And eaten, thought itself sweeter than e'er :
Was not a nightingale's bosom its bier ?
        Its sweetness must have indeed been rare
        To make the music so passing fair.

XIII.

Had the lot of the hothouse rose more good ;
    To be to the great and glorious dear,
To be tenderly tended while it stood,
        And when its petals fell, shrunk and sere,
        In a lord's bosom to have its bier ?

XIV.

Or that of the dog-rose, that grew in the wood ;
    To hedges and ditches and delver dear,
That tended itself, and grew as it would,
        And when its petals fell, shrunk and sere,
        In a nightingale's bosom had its bier?

XV.

I know not.   But for the hothouse rose,
    The fire in his bosom might have died
For lack of fuel, ere he might disclose
        The love that was life—the love that, denied,
        Had kill'd him, and, if not utter'd, his bride.

H

XVI.

And, but for the hip of the wild dog-rose,
 The nightingale might have starv'd and died :
Her sweetest carol might never disclose
 The pitiful boon that, if denied
 Her search, the fountain of music had dried.

L'Envoi.

Whether the wild or hothouse rose
 Did more good in their little day,
Only the God that made them knows ;
 He made them their own parts to play,
He gave their goodness, and took it away.
 Whether the lord or nightingale
 Did more good in their little day,
God only knows who made us all ;
 He made them their own parts to play ;
Let them rest in peace, they have pass'd away.

RAVENNA.

Ravenna, home of greatness not thine own,
Strange are the revolutions thou hast known
Since the Thessalian set thee by the deep
And gave thee to the Umbrian to keep.
Roman, Herulian and Ostrogoth
Foster'd thy budding vigour in its growth;
Byzantium and Lombardy and France
Cull'd but neglected thy luxuriance;
Romagniac, Venetian and Pope
Have let thy foliage fall and sap dry up.
　　From thee great Cæsar rose to win the world;
Where now thy forest stands Augustus furl'd
The broad sails of the galleys in his port;
To thee did weak Honorius resort,
And 'neath thy ramparts name and fame forego
To steal a slavish safety from the foe.
Here glorious Odoacer strove and died;
And here Theodoric the world defied,
But set a sample nought can e'er efface

H 2

Of toleration to a conquer'd race,˺
Marr'd only by the madness of his end
And this was due to treachery of friend,
Ingratitude of humour'd bigotry
And venomous relentless enmity.
His tomb and palace have not vanish'd yet ;
Who shall their mighty occupant forget?

Thy capture serv'd but to enhance thy fame,
For Belisarius took thee and became
A warning, for his loyalty and fate,
To those who might but will not be too great.
The very exarchs could not wholly quench
The embers of thy glory, nor the French,
Though those paid out thy homage to the East
And these bestow'd thine empire on a priest.

Though less renown'd in Europe's history
What name glows brighter in thy pedigree
Than Guido da Polenta, he who brought
The exile not yet famous to his court,
And drew Giotto from the Arno's side
To hallow and commemorate his pride
And foresight to all ages : he, too, gave
His child to Gianciotto and the grave.
O Interest, Ambition, Avarice,
Will votaries and victims ne'er suffice?
Must wistful-eyed Francesca too be given,

And Paolo's young heart and hopes be riven?
Must beauty wed misshapen affluence?
Tempt not poor beauty with a bald pretence :
Much of the sad Arturian legendry,
Ravenna's sweetest child, foreshadows thee :
Hadst heard of Tristram and dark Iseult? No,
Nor knewst thou Paolo for Paolo,
But thoughtst him Gianciotto. Tristram went
By Marc the king to Irish Iseult sent
To lead her to the surge-beat Cornish strand,
As should befit the lady of the land.
Paolo woo'd thee in his brother's name,
And yet the dear disaster was the same.
But after, when thou readst 'the cursed book,'
Didst ever think of Tristram? He would look
At Iseult as thy Paolo look'd at thee,
She Tristram as thou Paolo. To me
Paolo is Tristram and not Lancelot.
'Twas in thy Father's house that Dante wrote
The immortal vision, may be in the room
Where thou wast won to thy delight and doom.

O second sire of poets and the tongue
Sweetest of living utterance for song,
Had each allusion, episode and line
Of that great comedy, well call'd divine,
Perish'd while still thy story did survive,
So long our love and thy renown would live.

In Florence streets a nine years boy survey'd
A little, fairy, crimson-kirtled maid,
And treasur'd the remembrance : years march'd by
And every day her beauty he would eye,
Not with the sensuous gaze of human love,
But such fond worship as one lifts above
To Mother Mary : and her pure fair heart
Took it as worship, and they stay'd apart.
She wedded and he wept : a gentle dame
Seeing him weep, and knowing how it came,
Wept at his weeping : he thereby was moved
To loving her, but deeming, if one loved
That worship would be sullied, took her not.—
Too utterly unworthy of her lot
Was she he wedded.   Meanwhile in the state
The poet slept, the patriot grew great.
Yet 'tis not in that greatness we delight,
But when in friendlessness he turn'd his flight
To thee, old town.   More glory hast thou won
By welcoming this helpless, hopeless one
Than all thy exarchs, emperors and kings
Conferred on thee with world-wide gatherings.
Few melancholy pictures have there been
As thy life at Ravenna :—fit the scene
For such a tragedy—a sad, slow life
After those years of civic stir and strife :
Under Polenta's kindly patronage
Here thou pourtrayedst on the vivid page

The hopes, the hates, the loves, the lore of years
By Memory told, writ by Regret in tears.
The birthplace of thy Poem was thy tomb,
And hither ever genius hath come
For inspiration : here Chateaubriand
Knelt by the door, and at thy feet anon
Lay Alfieri : here that other one,
Noble as thou, and lone as thou wert lone,
A richer tribute laid upon thy hearse—
The volumes of his own immortal verse.
Justly may he be deem'd thy counterpart,
So like thee and unlike in his great heart,
Statesman and soldier had he felt the cause,
Exile and poet and lovelorn he was :
He, too, was a boy-wooer : he, too, woo'd
A maid who knew no corresponding mood,
His neighbour also : happy, too, had she
Receiv'd his unacknowledged fealty.
He, too, did wed another, as thy wife,
Destin'd to be the checkmate of his life :
Spurn'd by his countrymen, like thee, he fled,
And in Ravenna found his earliest stead.
He, too, denied a wife's or friend's relief,
Took refuge in his greatness from his grief,
Happier than thee in this, that here he found
A heart that touch'd his own, nor sought to wound.

Sweet Guiccioli, though cold hearts condemn

A passion that was not vouchsafed to them,
Envy and calumny are silenc'd now,
And dear to every Englishman art thou,
For softening the sufferings of him
Driven from home and household by a whim
Of that ungenerous prude he made his wife.
Had he but known thee earlier, his life
Had been a calmer passage, and thy name
As dear to virtue as it is to fame :
Soft be the slumbers of that golden head
And golden heart, wherever they be laid.

There is, Ravenna, in thy very air
A something breathing of the frail and fair.
Here Galla's beauty stemm'd the Gothic tide,
And here Francesca loved, and fell, and died ;
Here Traversara yielded long ago,
And Guiccioli sooth'd a poet's woe.

Here, too, is the Pineta Dante loved ;
Tradition points where oftenest he roved ;
Here pass'd the spectre-hunt Boccaccio told
And Dryden sang : and here the waters roll'd
That gave thy name, Chiassi : now the pine
Waves where the mast once bent above the brine.

Within one fane a hundred prelates lie ;
Another with Sofia's self might vie ;

Thy grand cathedral glows with Guido's art :
All that Giotto's genius could impart
Of beauty and imperishable worth
On Santa Maria's frescoes is set forth.

Hard by without the walls on that red plain
France and Ferrara shock the might of Spain :
Full seldom hath such greatness graced affray,
Here Pedro, here Coloura stood at bay,
Here, sorely press'd, Balthazar scorn'd to fly,
And Ariosto learn'd his chivalry ;
Small wonder that he came to sing it well
Who fought where Bayard fought and Nemours fell.

Enough ! Ravenna needeth not our praise,
Long since hath she been crown'd with deathless bays ;
Enough that Alfieri hail'd the spot,
And her two legends quaint Boccaccio wrote,
That Dryden, Hunt, and Rogers celebrate
Her beauties, and her children, and their fate;
And that of all the haunts of his unrest
Her lonely woods and walls pleased Juan best.
Be this Ravenna's glory and her pride,
That here lov'd Byron and here Dante died.

BOTTOM'S DREAM.

A BALLAD.

BOTTOM (*awaking*),—'When my cue comes, call me, and I will answer: my next is "Most fair Pyramus." Heigh-ho ! Peter Quince ! Flute, the bellows-mender ! Snout, the tinker ! Starveling ! God's my life ! Stolen hence and left me asleep! I have had a most rare vision. I have had a dream—past the wit of man to say what dream it was : man is but an ass, if he go about to expound this dream. Methought I was—there is no man can tell what. Methought I was—and methought I had —but man is but a patched fool, if he will offer to say what methought I had. The eye of man hath not heard, the ear of man hath not seen, man's hand is not able to taste, his tongue to conceive, nor his heart report, what my dream was. I will get Peter Quince to write *a ballad of this dream :* it shall be called *Bottom's Dream,* because it hath no bottom : and I will sing it in the latter end of a play, before the Duke : peradventure, to make it the more gracious, I shall sing it at her death.'—' Midsummer Night's Dream,' Act iv. Scene 1.

I am only a humble weaving clown,
As humble as any in Theseus' town,
And of maidens saw I never a one
But was marr'd with labour and brown with sun ;

Save the beautiful maiden captive led
That Theseus our duke to-morrow will wed,
And the daughter of Nedar and Egeus' may
Fair Helen and berry-brown Hermia.

Yestere'en I did dream such a dream I ween
As weaving craftsman may never have seen,
Though bewitch'd with faery glamourie,
A dream that the gods would be fain to see.

Carpenter Quince, and Starveling, and Snout,
And I, Flute, and Snug the joiner, did out
In the forest unseen to con a play
To greet the duke on his marriage day.

When the play had begun there stole a sprite
And over my head with fingering light
Slipp'd a something all heavy, and soft, and strong,
With leathery muzzle, and ears full long.

My companions flouted me and fled,
All glaring and gazing upon my head;
But I wandering up and down the glade
Sang out to show I was never afraid.

> ' The ouzel cock so black of hue,
>   With orange-tawny bill,
> The throstle with his note so true,
>   The wren with tiny quill.'

Then I dream'd in my dream that I fell asleep
And lay in a slumber full long and deep,
And I dream'd in my dream that I'd a dream
That kings in their castles would fairy deem.

For I dream'd of a woman goodly and fair,
With glittering tangles of golden hair ;
She had beautiful eyes of tender blue,
As sheen as the sunlight, as damp as dew.

She had ankles were slim, and round, and white,
Her feet were arching, and little, and light ;
Her lips were roses fresh from a shower,
Her body a delicate, dainty flower ;

With the garments of gods might well compare
Her raiment all royal, and rich, and rare,
On her beautiful tresses, bare and bright,
Was mirror'd in gold the silvery light.

She'd a voice like a dove, as soft and sweet,
A laugh like a rivulet rippling fleet,
And a kiss full as long and as loath to leave
As the sun when he sinks on a summer eve.

Then around me endearing arms she threw,
And swore that she loved me, tender and true ;
Made me glad with her kisses and her sighs,
And look'd full lovingly into my eyes.

But as bolder I grew, I kiss'd her oft,
And took up her body, so slim and soft,
And I swore that we never again should part,
As I clasp'd her hungrily home to my heart.

And for each of my kisses she gave me two,
And evermore kinder and kinder grew ;
And for every vow of troth I swore,
She gave me four kisses, and sware me four.

And my life till now seem'd a dream of pain,
And I swore that I never would dream again ;
When a-sudden a man as goodly and fair,
With the same bright raiment and eyes and hair,

Advanc'd to my lady, and, drawing near,
Look'd at her full kindly, and call'd her dear,
And begg'd her to give him the Indian boy
That long he had listed to be his joy ;

Then weeping she threw both her arms round him
And, casting her body so fair and slim
On the violet-bed before his feet,
Craved pity with pleading lowly and sweet,

While she promis'd the little Indian boy,
That she loved so fondly, to be his joy,
This, and anything else that he might fain,
So he would make her his lady again.

Then he kiss'd her, and swore a termless truce,
And open'd her eyes with the magic juice.
And with loathing she shrunk from me and wept,
Beholding the monster with whom she slept.

Then he laugh'd in shrill sweet scorn at her luck
And blowing his horn for his henchman Puck,
Bade him take the enchantment off my head,
And, ere I could open my eyes, they fled.

When the sun on my eyelids streaming down
Awoke me, I knew me a weaving clown ;
I had slept out the night i' the woods, I knew,
For all my garments were sodden with dew.

You may tell me my dream is false or true,
It will sate my longing my long life through,
For no daughter of toil and moil shall e'er
Fill arms that feel they have handled my fair.

WILD FLOWERS.

I.

Two boy nobles on a day
Spied a bank with blossoms gay,
Where in rival sweetness met
Forget-me-not and violet,
Peach-hued wild geraniums,
Foxes'-gloves with rosy gums ;
Daisies pied, red, white and blue,
Roses wild of ev'ry hue,
Crimson, cream, and creamy white,
Ragged Robins bold and bright ;
Harebells ringing fairy knells
Back to Canterbury bells,
Buttercups of glossy gold,
Clover-clusters manifold,
Mayweed, monk's-hood and cornflow'rs
All in honeysuckle bowers ;
Thistles and a dozen others,
Less belov'd and lovely brothers.
   Robin pull'd a violet
Trembling, tearful, dewy-wet,

Wild Flowers.

Shrinking from his wanton grasp
Fragranter at ev'ry gasp.
Dickon pluck'd a wild fair rose
That her charms would fain expose,
Opening her ev'ry sweet
For the fickle winds to meet.
Tenderly he took the blossom
To his loyal, loving bosom,
Tho' her prickles drew the blood
From his tender fingerhood.
　Hot and dusty was the day,
Long and weary was the way.
Unaccustom'd to such fare,
Both were tir'd and cross with care.
Ravish'd from her cool and calm,
Hot and huddled in his palm,
Robin's blossom hung her head,
All her beauty shrunk and shed.
Robin, when he saw her fade,
Call'd the drooping flower a jade,
Flung her on the dusty road,
Live or languish, as she could.
Dickon cried him shame to thieve
If he after meant to leave.
Only a wild flow'r, you say,
Yet she spent her little day,
All her childhood's sunny space,
All her girlhood and her grace,

All her love and loveliness,
All her truth and tenderness,
Simply as you most enjoy'd
When your sensual greed is cloy'd,
You leave her in the dust to die,
And hurry on unheedingly.

And Dickon's, on his bosom laid,
Soon afterward began to fade :
The prickles scratch'd, and sorely bled
The tender flesh that was their bed.
But Dickon kept them bravely there
Though they were sharp and it was bare.
Though thou art old and overblown
And graceless, now thy beauty's flown,
Still all the graces that were thine
And all thy youthful charms were mine ;
And shame it were now these are gone
To leave thy helpless age alone.

II.

Earl Robert woo'd a village maid,
The sweetest lass in all the glade,
With tress of black, and eye of brown,
And long love-lashes drooping down,
As beautiful, and dark, and **sweet**,
And modest as a violet.

I

He took her, as of old he took
That other violet from the nook,
Because her fair virginity
Was pleasing to his wanton eye,
Although he lov'd her in his bosom
No better than of old the blossom.
Long time he woo'd the maid in vain,
Till, by his birth and beauty ta'en,
She thought his selfish fears were just,
And lent her honour to his lust.
Thus liv'd she long a happy life,
Unconscious that he had a wife,
And dreaming that their nuptial bed
Was some day to be hallowed.
But when her beauty and his youth
Departing told the bitter truth,
He cast her off to sin, or die
In loneliness and misery.

III.

Earl Richard woo'd an actress fair,
As beautiful as debonnaire ;
Her hair rich rippling, brown in hue,
Her eye of moving mirthful blue,
As lissome and as sweetly free
As any wild woodbine could be,

As graceful as the maiden-hair,
As fair as any flower is fair,
But light and wantonsome withal,
And loving to be lov'd by all.
As fond of roving as a rose,
As open to each breeze that blows,
With full as many spines in wrath
As any hedge-row briar hath.
Earl Richard woo'd her—nor in vain,
Some eminence she 'd long'd to gain.
He lov'd her as he lov'd his life,
Yet did not vow to make her wife :
For this he knew, that great estates
Should have great ladies for their mates.
But though his Rose's nuptial bed
With no due rites was hallowed,
She had no rival in his love,
Nor suffer'd he his thoughts to rove,
But gave her all devotion
That can from honest hearts be won.
  Unworthy his fidelity,
With spiteful fits of jealousy,
And sighing after other loves,
Rosie her lover's anger moves,
And often to that kindly breast
Full thorny is the flow'r he's press'd.

IV.

A few years pass, and Rose's face
A blighting fever doth deface.
Then, too, she feels, her fairness fled,
That she will soon be brought to bed.
    Earl Richard, tho' her beauty paled,
Ever was fonder as she ail'd,
And sat beside her many day
While on her feverish bed she lay.
A look of grateful tenderness,
A feeble smile, a faint caress,
Was ample pay for present care
And former doubting and despair.
And often would he stoop to soothe
Her poor scarr'd face with tender mouth.
But ever on her grew the fear
That, now her summer-bloom was sere,
He'd cast her off and take a wife,
And lead, they'd say, a better life,
Or find a younger, lovelier one,
Now that her loveliness was gone.
So one day, when with kindly grasp
Her wasted fingers he would clasp,
She lean'd her graceful golden head
Against his shoulder close, and said,
Timorously and tearfully,
In tones that sounded like a sigh,

'Richard' : he look'd at her and clutch'd
The little lean white hands he touch'd
Closer, as tho' they wish'd to part,
And whisper'd back, 'Speak on, sweetheart.'
'Richard,' said she, ' my beauty's gone.
The pain I've given you, I own ;
You have been very kind to me,
And I as unkind as might be.
The time has come for us to part,
I can no longer rule your heart.
Some younger, with a fairer face,
Must have my power and my place,
And earn it with a gentler grace ;
Or you will wed some highborn dame,
To breed succession to your name.
But grant one favour ere I go,
'Tis right and time for you to know
That I shall be a mother soon ;
Let not the clouds that crush my noon
Smother the dawning of my child ;
Nor let its young life be defil'd
With gutter wantonness and want.
Tho' now my claims on you are scant,
I ask you by what love you owe
For sweet embraces long ago,
And ev'ry dear remember'd kiss,
And all our passion and our bliss,
To free it from this bitter yoke,

And in the ways of gentle folk
To breed it up, and when you see
Its childish sweetness, think of me.'
 Earl Richard kiss'd away a tear,
And said, ' Poor darling, have no fear :
Why talk to me so timidly?
I have no mind to lay thee by.
Tho' bound not by a marriage vow,
Thou art as dear as ever now ;
Nay, dearer, seeing that the loss
Of one poor beauty—beauty's dross
Had power to make thee feel the more.
In youth, I own, I set a store
On such poor wares, but now I see
A hundred other charms in thee.
I love the fitful smiles and tears,
The childlike pouts and girlish fears ;
I love the little nestling form
That nestles—when it dreads a storm.
I like the very jealousy
And sighs that do not breathe for me.
What makes your tender moods so dear
Is that they are not always here :
Caresses deal a daintier pride
To those to whom they're oft denied.
Love without check or change doth cloy,
Variety is part of joy.
But, Pretty, soothe your mother's heart,

For you and I will never part.
Your child shall be of gentle birth,
⁺ For ere you bring our darling forth,
We will be join'd for love and life,
For you shall be my wedded wife.'

MY AUNT.

I don't think Aunt was ever young ;
I'm sure she never will be old :
    She's far too stately for the one
    And sprightly for the other.
    Shelley wrote verses to his son
    And Cowper on his mother,
      But yet I'm sure you can't
Find any poet who has sung,
    Or anecdotist who has told
      The virtues of an Aunt.

The aunt I praise is very tall,
    Her cheeks are wrinkleless and fair,
    Her features fine and regular,
    Her figure most majestic,
    Her mien and manners courtly are,
    Her habits are domestic.
      Go far and near, you can't
From nine to ninety, all in all,
    Find any woman to compare
      One moment with my Aunt.

She'll travel all and ev'ry day
　On railway or in diligence ;
　　And let no murmur pass her lip
　　　For forty hours together ;
　　She's never sick on any ship
　　　In any kind of weather.
　　　　Try what you will, you can't
Find any project to dismay,
　Or any journey too immense
　　　And difficult for Aunt.

Two years ago—I do not know
　Exactly what her age might be,—
　　She did the whole of Palestine
　　　From Beyrout down to Joppa,
　　Italy, Egypt, and the Rhine :
　　　The brigands couldn't stop her
　　　　Exploring Greece : you can't,
From John o' Groats to Jericho,
　Find any curiosity
　　　Unvisited by Aunt.

At Christmastide her hands are full
　For all the poor : she always sends
　　Material remembrances
　　　To nephews and to nieces :
　　If she has any fault, it is
　　　That woman's heart increases

The nephews' share : you can't
Find any Lady Bountiful
As dear alike to poor and friends
As my especial Aunt.

WESTWARD HO!

A MAIL-DAY RHYME.

I.

Westward Ho! the east winds blow
  Athwart the Indian sea,
And westward ho the ship doth go
  That beareth news to thee.
But yesternight I dream'd I came
  Unto my father's hall;
The quickset hedges were the same
  And the ivy on the wall.

II.

The house stood open and I saw
  My sister on the stair;
She call'd my father to the door,
  And I embrac'd him there.
A brother and a sister came
  In answer to her call;
The quickset hedges were the same
  And the ivy on the wall.

III.

They talk'd apace, and laugh'd apace,
  And loud the laughter grew,
And then they look'd me in the face
  And said 'twas bronzed in hue ;
Then asked me of the strange south seas
  Where I had been so long,
And of the swarthy savages
  That I had dwelt among.

IV.

So laugh'd we and so chatted we
  The sun adown the sky,
Then spent the night in jovial glee
  Until the sun was high.
It was a dream.   I stand to-day
  'Neath an Australian sun ;
The bower-birds were out at play
  This morning on the run.

V.

It was a dream ; I was not there,
  Nor aught of home I saw ;
No sister stood upon the stair,
  No father at the door.

But westward ho the east winds blow
   Athwart the Indian sea,
And westward ho the ship doth go
   That beareth news of me.

ON A BIRTHDAY CARD.

A birthday offering,
A little one I bring;
Yet do not it despise,
 For it hath come from far,
From one whose pathway lies
 Beneath the southern star.
It comes to tell you this,
 That, though too far apart
For lip and lip to kiss,
 Yet heart can cling to heart;
And therefore do I bring
 This little offering.

IN MEMORIAM C. LE *F.*

BORN AT GRASMERE, CUMBERLAND, KILLED IN AFGHAN-
ISTAN.

Wandering over the Cumbrian mountains,
  Herding his flocks on Helvellyn's breast,
Watering sheep at the hillside fountains
  The high young spirit could find no rest.

Galloping over Australian meadows
  On the fierce steed that he loved the best,
Only the flickering gum-tree shadows
  'Twixt him and the sun—he found no rest.

Under the sky on the Afghan mountains
  With a foeman's bullet in his breast,
Dead for a draught of the hillside fountains
  To quench his fever—he lies at rest.

ETHEL.

Katie is a pretty shrew ;
Isabel a little blue ;
Maud as proud as Lucifer ;
Christobel a sonneteer ;
Edith is reserv'd and fair ;
Eleanor hath auburn hair ;
Margaret is masculine ;
I don't care for Adeline ;
Beatrix is very sweet,
And hath many at her feet ;
Nothing hath she ever harm'd,
But an iceberg's sooner warmed ;
She's so dully temperate
That she cannot even hate ;
All her useful life is spent
In the tedious content
That in story-books befalls
Angels and good animals.
Mary is a peacemaker,
All the people round love her,

And I love her passively,
But she is too good for me.
Daring Ethel is a queen,
Most majestic in her mien
And most royal in her ways ;
All the men her beauty praise,
Not before her royal face
If they dread condign disgrace,
Admiration in your eyes
Is her look'd-for, lawful prize ;
Admiration in your speech
Is a statutable breach
Of Her Grace's social code.
No one ever waltz'd or rode,
Shot an arrow or a glance,
With more finish'd elegance ;
Neither is she over-bold,
Callous, feelingless, nor cold.
If she sees a rough young squire
Reeling backwards from the fire
Of a merciless coquette
For his uncouth etiquette,
She will cross a crowded room
To alleviate his doom,
Make him come and sit by her,
Be a smiling listener
To the ' bag ' of yesterday,
Where the warmest corners lay

K

In the Earl of Foxshire's woods ;
How his blood-mare swam the floods,
Of the row with Farmer Scroggs,
And the names of all the dogs.
And if talk-about is true
Ethel can be tender too.
Who remembers Dick Duval,
Once the favourite of all ?
Honest, hearty, handsome Dick,
Brave, and generous, and quick,
But there was no runagate
Ever so unfortunate.
Dicky never could escape,
As a schoolboy, from a scrape ;
Dick was never in a brawl
But he came off worst of all ;
He, whose share was often least,
Bore the blame of all the rest.
Dick at last—it ne'er appear'd
Why or wherefore—was cashier'd,
Driven from his father's hall,
Scowl'd upon and shunn'd by all.
Dick to queenly Ethel came :
Ethel had no word of blame,
Did not turn away or frown,
Ask'd no explanation,
Wrung his slack hand heartily,
And, looking at him earnestly,

In a sweet firm whisper said :
' I can trust you, Dick ; you did
Nothing base, or mean, or low ;
What you did I do not know.
Do not tell me—only say
That you would not turn away
From a man who did the same
As from one whose touch was shame.
While a tear splash'd in the dust,
' Bless you, Ethel, for your trust,'
Was the broken-voic'd reply ;
' Never such a thing did I.
But I came to say good-bye :
I am going to the East,
Under Osman to enlist,
From my name to wipe the stain,
And retrieve fair fame again.'
' Dick, I will not bid you stay,
Go and wipe the stain away.
One thing promise me, that you
Nothing in despair will do.
Try to come safe home again,
You have one who will remain
E'er your firm and faithful friend.
Promise, Dick, and try to mend,
No more getting into scrapes,
No more hazardous escapes,

Saving when you face the foe,
But then do as brave men do :
Wait until the battle—then
Give your gallant heart the rein ;
And, if you have time to write,
Send the story of a fight
Bravely fought and bravely won,
How you are, and what you've done;
Saying when, your penance o'er,
You are coming home once more,
And where letters will reach you.'
' Who will write them, if I do ?'
' I myself, Dick.' ' You will ?' ' Yes,
I do not desert distress.'
' And can you, who are so fair,
Coveted by all men, care—
Stoop to correspond with me?'
'Correspond ? Yes, certainly.
Dick, I place you far before,
All the faultless fools who bore
One to death with etiquette ;
Who have nothing to regret,
Not because no ill they've wrought,
But because they've not done aught
Saving sleep, and drink, and eat
And I hold the manly heat
That lands you in scrape and stain
Far above the force of brain

That leads some men to apply
Lifetimes to philosophy,
In contempt of common things—
Births, and loves, and buryings.
You've been hearty to excess,
But I like you none the less.'
' Hear me, Ethel, I am mad,
But I am not wholly bad ;
I am mad, but going away
For long months, perhaps for aye.
Hear me, Ethel, long have I
Loved you most devotedly :
In the days when I was heir
To the acres broad and fair
Which are mine no longer now,
In the bright days of my youth
And wild days of later growth.
But you ever seem'd too good,
Of too queenly womanhood,
And too wonderful to be
For a simple man like me.
Hear me, Ethel, ere I go,—
Hear me,—I would have you know
That I love you as none can
But a passion-ridden man.
Hear me : if I live to come,
With refurbish'd honour, home,

And you e'er should need my aid,
If in life-blood it were paid,
I would shed it every drop
To give you a minute's hope.
But if I should never come,
Try to clear my name at home.
I will write you all the tale
Of this last scrape while I sail.
Good-bye, Ethel : do you weep?
Tears for worthier sorrows keep ;
I'm not worth a single tear
From your lashes.   Ethel dear,
Darling Ethel, do not cry.'
'Wait, Dick, do not say good-bye,
I love you too : if you still
Wish to marry me, I will
Wish to marry you, love.'   'No,
Not when I have sunk so low ;
You who seemed too good for me
In my old prosperity.
Darling, you would stoop too far,
Fair and noble as you are.
I am, do I what I can,
A dishonourable man.'
'Not dishonourable, Dick ;
Ills have fallen fast and thick
On your wild, unlucky head,
But I know you truly said

You've not done since you were born
What would make you shrink in scorn
From a man who'd done the same,
As from one whose touch was shame.
Dick, you shall not leave me thus.'
' You are over-generous.'
' If I may not be your wife
I'll be single all my life ;
But I will not bid you stay
Till the stain is wip'd away
By good service bravely done
On the field of action ;
But when you come home again
I'll be yours if you are fain.'

   Dick look'd at her wistfully.
' Ethel, is this charity—
Just your nobleness of heart,
Seeing all my friends depart
But yourself—or is it true? '
' True : I always have loved you ;
But if you had come to me
In your wild prosperity
Then I should have answer'd, No,
Not until you've learn'd to show
What good stuff you're moulded of.
When you've proven this, enough,

I will gladly be your wife.
But while all you do is rife
With outrage and escapade,
I would sooner be a maid.
Now, you do not need advice,
But the light of loving eyes.'

   ' Sweet, this generosity
Too heroic is for me ;
I can't be so generous
As to once again refuse
Such a crown of love as this.
Darling Ethel, let me kiss
Your kind hand before I go.'
' Let you kiss my hand, Dick !   No :
Kiss my lips ; they're not too good
For a brave man : spare your blood
And spare life whene'er you may,
Strike home on a doubtful day ;
If you can write to me, try ;
Good-bye, dear old Dick, good-bye ! '

   This is Ethel's mystery,
No one knows it all but me.
Ethel bearded Squire Duval
In his study at the hall,
Told him Dick was not to blame,
But his answer was the same.

' Dick's disgraced an ancient line,
He's no longer son of mine.'
But there's nought he will not do,
If Queen Ethel asks him to,
Saving this ; and on a day,
After Ethel's gone away,
He will say, with almost joy,
' She did not desert my boy.'

When you look upon her face,
In her beauty you can trace
Something wistful now and then ;
Then she turns and smiles again
On her waiting worshippers :
They know not this spur of hers
Press'd against her noble heart,
And, when bootless they depart,
Mutter slanders of coquette.
I myself should not know yet
Were it not that Dick and I
Were school-cronies formerly,
Shared a study and a crib,
Had a fight : I broke his rib,
He made music in my head.
When he went away, he said :
' Ethel, I've told all to Fred ;
He and I are limb and limb,
Make a confidant of him

Ethel.

When you want to talk of me.
This is how I came to be
Privy to her sacrifice.
Often, with her grave sweet eyes,
Fasten'd on me, she will ask
Me of every trick and task
Of his scapegoat schoolboy life.
He is worthy such a wife ;
Try your best, you will not find
Better fellow of his kind.
He'd have been a famous knight
In the bright enchanted night
Of Provençal chivalry.
Modern-times reality,
Like a dull unwelcome day,
Drove the magic night away
With its legendary grace.
When I look upon her face,
Making Dick a schoolboy Cid,
Rubbing up the feats he did,
And her grateful fluent eyes
Give me eloquent replies,
Oft I wish that I might plead
Someone else's cause instead.

But I have a pet as well,
Lovely, laughing, light-heart Nell.
We don't talk of love, but play
At it all and every day :

I steal kisses and she laughs,
Swear they're earnest, and she chaffs.
Once, when I contrived to go
Underneath the mistletoe,
Saying she'd a score to pay,
She kiss'd me and tripp'd away,
Not too quickly to be caught,
And with well-feign'd struggles brought
Underneath the bough once more.
We've had quarrels o'er and o'er,
But we always make it up,
Neither cares to sulk or mope.
    If my sisters hint that I
Feel for Nellie tenderly,
I'm indignant, and retort,
From a well-assur'd report,
Of Sir This, and Captain That,
Giving tits for every tat.
    If her cousin, Bertie Bell,
Whispers spitefully to Nell,
'Nellie, you're in love with Fred,'
She will toss her pretty head,
And, with mock humility,
Drop a curtsey and reply,
'Well, and if your charge were true,
Better far with Fred than you.'
All the same one's fidgety
When the other is not by.

We engage at ev'ry ball
For the waltzes one and all :
Waltzing's too divine a dance
To be left to common chance ;
You should only waltz with one
In such perfect unison
With you, as you cannot get
Save you often practise it :
Squares we always give away.
When it's supper time, we stay
'Till the extras all are done,
Then we go and sup alone,
Make the mottoes vehicles
For the truths one never tells
Without such occasion.
Whispering we linger on
Until we away are sent
Or slip into sentiment ;
Then we go and waltz again
Feeling fire in ev'ry vein :
Nellie shuts a blithe blue eye
In delicious ecstasy,
As we float (we hate to haste),
And I clasp her slender waist
With a more expressive arm.
Sweet abandon is her charm :
Nellie looks her loveliest
When the sunny elf-locks, press'd

In the heavy plaits behind,
Play the truant in the wind,
And the errand-blushes stay
And don't hurry straight away
Soon as they have said their say.

Ev'ry Christmas here we meet
At my father's country seat,
Staying for a month or more :
Ev'ry Christmas, when it's o'er,
Many wish it would begin
And think breaking-up a sin.
Nell and I are worst of all,
We'd like Christmas day to fall
Once a month : and now I find
That I must make up my mind ;
For we clearly can't go on
In the way we've always done ;
Nellie will be eighteen soon,
I was twenty-one in June.

Χάρις ἄχαρις.

In lofty halls, 'mid flowers of richest dye
   And subtle fragrance stealing through each sense
   As 'twere a harbinger of somnolence,
On couch of silken web behold her lie,
A daughter of our old nobility,
   Whose beauty is their birthright,—fair of face,
   Herself a sweet embodiment of grace
And portrait of a poet's fantasy.

As in a haze :—hast never had a dream
   In which thy lot was, such as hers, to be
   For e'er becalmed in an enchanted sea
Of never-ruffled Pleasure, where no beam
Of light convicts the darkness, no winds seem
   To coax a wave, or belly out the sail,
   To waft the mariners beyond the pale
Of that dead life, their being to redeem ?

She never knew a sorrow : all her days
   Have been the haunt of pleasure and sweet rest :
   No trouble ever harrowed that white breast,
But loving hands have smoothed the softest ways
For her to tread : no murmur but of praise
   Hath woo'd an echo in her ear, but still
   Ne'er to the brim life's goblet doth she fill,
For all her joys are veiled as in a haze.

Such is her life : but the electric flow
   Of gladness welling from a joyous heart,
   The leaping pulse, the truer, better part
Of this dear life,—these in her never glow :
He gets not joy who hath not gotten woe :
   But as the silly flies in summer hours,
   Tranced by the opiate essence of the flowers,
Drain a full cup of bliss, nor bliss doth know.

FROM THE DRAMA OF 'CHARLES II.'

REFRAIN.

Come and kiss me, mistress Beauty,
I will give you all that's due t'ye.

I will taste your rosebud lips
Daintily as the bee sips ;
At your bonny eyes I'll look
Like a scholar at his book :

On my bosom you shall rest,
Like a robin on her nest :
Round my body you shall twine,
I'll be elm, and you be vine :

In a bumper of your breath
I would drain a draught of death :
In the tangles of your hair
I'd be hang'd and never care.

Then come kiss me, mistress Beauty,
I will give you all that's due t'ye.

TO A YOUNG LADY.

Slowly but surely, surely but slowly
You my heart-errant have vanquish'd most throughly;
  Sweet, you are beautiful,
  I think you dutiful,
Modest and maidenly, loving and lowly.

Sprightly and slender, slender and sprightly,
Tell me who foots it so featly and lightly?
  Hath any maiden fair
  Such a wise noble air?
Can other eyes beam both sagely and brightly?

Airy and artless, artless and airy,
Flitting about like a midsummer fairy,
  Pride from your presence flies,
  Love at your mercy lies;
Prythee, be merciful, Mary, my Mary.

L

TO A VILLAGE BEAUTY.

Little lowly violet,
  Beautiful, and sweet, and dark,
When with dew thy cheeks are wet
  Then thy sweetness most we mark.

Gentle maiden, dark and sweet,
  Beauty ne'er so much we prize,
Charms are never so complete
  As when tears are in the eyes.

Maiden, like the violet,
  Beautiful, and dark, and sweet,
Farthest off from fear and fret
  Is the lowliest retreat.

PITY IS AKIN TO LOVE.

Valour fain would go a-wooing ;
  Wit would teach him how to woo ;
Fame would speed him in his suing ;
  Love encourage him to sue.
    Valour, with his henchmen three,
    Hied to Beauty merrilie.

Valour blurted out his passion ;
  Fame extoll'd his high renown ;
Love *his* comeliness's fashion ;
  Wit, more courtly, Beauty's own.
    All in vain—unheeding them,
    Beauty would have none of him.

Valour flew in wrath to battle ;
  Wit could not avert defeat ;
Love abhorr'd the rack and rattle,
  Fame the stigma of retreat.
    Wit, Love, Fame no longer nigh,
    Valour laid him down to die.

Beauty, cause of all his sighing,
   Tripping past the field of strife,
As her lover lay a-dying,
   Lost her heart and saved his life ;
      A change of tack which goes to prove
      That Pity is akin to Love.

Whilst yet the calm hours creep
Dream thou, and from thy sleep
Then wake to weep.

SHELLEY—*Mutability.*

Oft in the noon of even,
    When I am in my bed,
A vision steals from heaven
    Of dear ones who are dead.

When they are here, I borrow
    Light heart from long ago,
And bid good-bye to sorrow
    And kiss my hand to woe.

But—heigh-ho—breaks the dawning ;
    My holidays are done ;
For memory comes with morning,
    And sorrow with the sun.

THE DEAD OLD YEAR.

Come, soul, and bury the dead old year,
    Time was when she was fair,
Though now her body be shrunk and sere,
    Gone the gold of her hair.

In the cathedral of memory,
    Set up with escutcheon meet,
And with her sisters the years gone by
    Give her embalming sweet.

A warm tear over her ashes drop,
    True wife was she to you,
She bore you many a darling hope,
    And blessings not a few.

Then saith he to his disciples, The harvest truly is plenteous, but the labourers are few ; pray ye therefore the Lord of the harvest, that he will send forth more labourers into his harvest. *St. Matthew*, IX., 37, 38.

I.

The harvest is ripe on orchard and plain,
The flush on the fruit, the gold on the grain ;
But the sun is hot, and the day is long,
The labourers neither many nor strong.

II.

There's a land is fair and a land is nigh,
And a rift of light in the stormy sky;
There are many on board who love their life,
But the sailors are few and worn with strife.

III.

The city is fair and the people great,
But few are the soldiers that guard the gate,
And the foe are many and threatening
To force the people away from their King.

IV.

Our home is fair and our Father is kind,
But the way is hidden and hard to find ;
And there's many a weary mile to go,
And there are not enow the way to show.

V.

O harvesters, gather ye in the grain ;
O mariners, bring us to port again ;
O warriors, guard the gate from the foe,
And guide us, O God, in the way to go.

SALOPIA INHOSPITALIS.

Touch not that maid ;
She is a flower, and changeth but to fade.
Fragrant is she, and fair
As any shape that haunts this lower air ;
In form as graceful and as free
As honeysuckles and the lilies be ;
Insensible, and shrinking from caress
As flowers, which you peril when you press.

Gaze not on her,
She is a being of another sphere.
Brilliant is she, and bright
As any star illuminate at night ;
Of stuff as sober and as fine
As hers whose glory through the moon doth shine ;
Unliker to come down to this thy love
Than any orb that's fixed for aye above.

Heed her no more,
She is a gem whose heart thou canst not bore ;
Glist'ring is she, and grand
As any stone that decks a monarch's hand ;
In face as free from flaw or stain
As diamond from mine, or pearl from main :
But she thy fire and fever never felt,
For adamant can neither waste nor melt.

CONFESSIO AMANTIS.

(AMATOR.   AMATA.   MATER.)

I.

By the boudoir fire we're sitting,
Shadows from the fire are flitting,
Creeping, crawling, sweeping, sprawling
O'er the ceiling ; night is falling
  On the dreary drizzling day ;
  Kettledrum is clear'd away.

II.

In the firelight eyes look brighter,
In the firelight cares are lighter,
In the firelight fair looks fairer,
In the firelight rare is rarer.
  Sunshine's only for the glad,
  Firelight can illume the sad.

III.

Half-past five : we dine at seven—
One clear hour at least is given.

Books in plenty : I must find one—
Why will memory remind one
    That one hasn't read a thing
    Since the other evening ?

IV.

'' 'Prenticeship of Wilhelm Meister,
As a tale-book, not the dry'st here ;
I can never understand it,
Could the master-mind that plann'd it ?
    Two small feet upon the mat
    Interest me more than that.

V.

' Poet at the Breakfast Table,'
Light, and vigorous, and able.
Why on earth will glances wander,
With attention four times fonder,
    To two little hands that clasp
    ' Enoch Arden ' in their grasp ?

VI.

Good ! here is the triple story—
Heaven, Hell, and Purgatory :
Darling Bice, brave old Dante,
Grace I crave for homage scanty ;
    You I cannot see to-night
    For a maiden opposite.

VII.

* Landor, thy beloved pages
Bridge th' abysm of the ages ;
Yet to-night they fail their duty ;
Through Aspasia's boasted beauty,
    As through misty morning air,
    Dawns a fair face over there.

VIII.

Let me look at something sterner,
Hallam, Stubbs, or Dawson Turner,—
'Grand Monarque,' or 'Reign of Terror,'
'Bess's Glory,' 'Charles's Error : '
    Each in dim confusion flies,
    Scared away by two blue eyes.

IX.

Love is lost in calculations—
Adam Smith on 'Wealth of Nations : '
Bees whose bags are full of money
Do not gather love as honey.
    Business, no admission there !
    What is gold to golden hair ?

X.

'Six-fifteen ! will you excuse me?'
'If your daughter won't refuse me

Help in solving calculations
Made while reading ' Wealth of Nations.'
' Nellie will enjoy it.'   Gone—
Nell and I are left alone !

XI.

' Westward Ho !' is vastly pretty,—
Burning Frank and Rose, a pity ;
Beautiful they look together
   Dying.   I'm not certain whether
    I could not be burnt, to see
    Somebody so close to me.

XII.

Nellie's very wrapt in reading ;
Diligence I hate impeding ;
Yet has she, for all that's wrapt her,
Not got through a single chapter.
    I must beg for Nellie's aid,
    Calculations to be made.

XIII.

' Three years past, come this December,
(You no doubt will not remember)
I, a schoolboy, loved you madly,
Talked of dying for you gladly ;
    Most of all, beyond compare
    I esteemed your eyes and hair.

XIV.

'Now your eyes look sweet and tender ;
Does the fireglow lend them splendour ?
And your hair shines richer golden ;
Is it to the flames beholden ?
  And your face looks very fair ;
  Have the embers influence there ?

XV.

' Nay, I swear I think you're blushing ;
Never fire made such a flushing.
And your eyes are bright and pelting ;
Never fire made such a melting.
  Would you take it very ill,
  If I said I loved you still ?

XVI.

' Sweet, if you must fall, my bosom
Shall receive the falling blossom.
If the tears must rain, the shower
Raining here will feed the flower.
  If your weakness need support,
  Nature made me stronger for't.

XVII.

' Kiss me, Nellie, I'll not owe it,—
No such banker as the poet ;

Nay, invest your fund of kissing—
Int'rest cent. per cent.—increasing.
    Tears and smiles, just one kiss more :
    Have you looked as fair before ? '

XVIII.

By the boudoir fire we're sitting ;
Shadows from the fire are flitting
O'er the ceiling.—Struck eleven !
Dinner's always sharp at seven.
    Goodness ! here is bed-time come,
    And we've never left the room.

WITH GOD.

I cannot deem I am with God,
  When in a shapeless, graceless room
  I hear the unmodulated boom
Of one who treads the byways trod

By all the sheepy, sleepy throng
  That follows in the wake of yore,
  And holds that what has been before,
The Church's right, can ne'er be wrong:

I cannot listen to the hum
  Of sing-song prayer, and harsh response,
  And dream that invitations
So coldly breath'd to God may come.

Sometimes in high cathedral choir,
  With 'storied windows richly dight,
  Casting a dim religious light,'
Or lit and live with sunset fire,

M

When one, who has the sweet clear tones
  That should be chosen to declare
  God's message, or with utter'd prayer,
To represent the kneeling ones

In silent worship wrapt, chants out
  Our solemn, tuneful liturgy,
  And all the choristers reply
With joyous and harmonious shout ;

Or when from God's New Testament
  He reads the troubles undergone
  By one who left a heavenly throne
Upon his Father's work intent ;

Of all his labours and his love,
  His selfless, ceaseless charity,
  And universal sympathy
With those who have no home above,

And no home here ; or when the strain
  Of the loud anthem peals as high
  As if it strove to pierce the sky,
Then sinks to human pitch again,

Sometimes my heart will swell and pant
  The while, with mystical delight,
  I scan existence infinite
And all the risks concomitant :

And sometimes on the ocean shore,
  * When nought of sight or sound were nigh,
   But for the awful rivalry
Of wind and wave in rush and roar ;

More often on a mountain-top,
   With no companion but the clouds,
   Or misty mantle that enshrouds
Its shoulder blades three quarters up :

But nearest earth God seems to be
   Deep in the stillness of a night,
   Cloudless, and passionless, and bright,
And voiceless but to such as me ;

He looks at me with starry eyes,
   And whispers with the waving leaves,
   And listens with the echoing eaves,
And sends a smile of paradise

Over the meek face of the moon.
   I commune with myself and him,
   With seeing heart and pupils dim
Until the daylight comes too soon.

COUSINS.

Out into the darkness poor Robert stept,
   It was chill enough, God knows, outside,
While within rich Dick in an armchair slept,
   The snug armchair by the warm fireside.

Out into the darkness of life stept he,
   It's chill enough, God knows, for the poor,
And draughts of its freezing reality
   Will sometimes steal 'neath a rich man's door.

Cousin Robert and I were never friends;
   We'd nothing in common save goodwill;
But strange, as to-night our acquaintance ends,
   To-night we both feel a friendly thrill.

Poor Robert is homely, simple, and plain,
   Knows not ambition, the crown, or curse,
But has the finest of all, to gain
   A mite for a widow'd mother's purse.

Out into the darkness poor Robert stept,
   My cousin Bob with his blithe good-night ;
The fire went out while the other slept,
   But the moon lit the wide dark world with light.

TO THE LATE MISS ADELAIDE NEILSON

ON HER IMPERSONATION OF JULIET.

I.

Dear was the hour and happy was the day,
    And quit the claim of genius on grace,
    When thou, the fairest of our English race,
The fairest race on earth, as all men say,
Didst venture, not unworthily, to play
    The sweetest maid his master-pen could trace,
    Whose faintest outline nothing shall efface—
Envy, nor wear of ages, nor essay
    Of mortal copy ever.   Shakspere stands
      On that vast fabric that he founded high
Above the waves of time, above the hands
      Of master architects, who fain would vie
With what his genius rear'd at his commands
      Aladdin-wise—no human masonry.

II.

And thou—thou hast the shape his mind conceiv'd,
   When he created Juliet, to ensure
   The love of gallant men, a face as pure
From fleck or flaw as hers was who believ'd
The tale the serpent whisper'd, and bereav'd
   Man of his home in Eden : to endure
   Was never maid's where flattery did lure ;
The fondest hearts were ever first deceived—
   Thine too perchance.   In beauty's fairest mould
     Thy face and form were cast : thou hast a lip
Would melt the rigour of Icelandic cold ;
     Thy limbs are of the deftest workmanship
That ever loving-worship did enfold
     Since Galatea felt his final chip,

III.

Who lov'd her into living : rings thy voice
   As sweetly as the nightingale who fills
   The lindens with the music of her trills
In summer, or the angels who rejoice
And harp their harmonies in Paradise ;
   Or like the becks that babble down the hills,
   Or like the winds that wail beside the sills
Of windows in old houses : no device

Is lacking to thy beauty's daintiness ;
   Genius has beam'd its brightest on thy brow,
And thou hast woman's glory, tumbling tress
   Down creamy neck and bosom and below,
And eyes that erring but too much confess
   As stars upon the southern heaven glow.

THE STING OF DEATH.

Glory banishes the terror
   That encompasses the grave ;
Hope of memory immortal
   Well might make a coward brave ;
And the great, whose birth or greatness
   Forces history to sing,
Find that Death has fail'd to conquer,
   And the tomb has lost its sting.

'Tis the numberless and nameless
   Taste the bitterness of death,
Those who feel that their remembrance
   Passes from them with their breath ;
Those whose worthiness and wisdom,
   And whose triumphs dearly won,
Are as fair and soon forgotten
   As a glimmer of the sun.

All their highest aspirations,
   All their widest hopes and aims,
Dreams of what should make the future,
   Shed a halo round their names;
All their envying and hatred,
   All their worshipping and love,
Are as lost as if the ocean
   Floated fathomless above.

AMOR ANNI.

IN ENGLAND.

In baby January
I met a little fairy,
Half-way in February
I woo'd : her name was Mary.

In March she was arch,
In April grew tender,
In May dawn'd the day,
In June the full splendour
Of a woman's love
Fill'd our common heaven ;
In July it throve,
August saw its even,
One September night
Starlit it fell sober,
Ever that poor light
Flicker'd in October.

Amor Anni.

Rheumatic old November
Quench'd its last smould'ring ember;
And when the year was dead
Even memory had fled.

LE ORDRE DE BEL EYSE.

1630.

First we love fair ladies,
   Then we love good books ;
Either have their virtues,
   Either have their vices ;
These are to divert us,
   Those are to entice us ;
Books outlive their pages,
   Ladies their good looks.

Next we love sweet music
   And the festive dance ;
Music makes us merry,
   Dancing glows with pleasure ;
Either salutary,
   Taken in good measure ;
Joy's the only physic
   That is worth its pence.

And we love good liquor,
　　Be it from the Rhine,
Cyder press'd in Devon,
　　Or fat college ale ;
Nectar's drunk in heaven,
　　Whisky by the Gael ;
Herrick—he's the Vicar—
　　Says they're all divine.

Last, and most devoutly
　　Love we a good friend,
One to mourn and miss us
　　When we've burst our bubbles,
Share in our successes,
　　And not shun our troubles.
Whoso does this stoutly,
　　Love him to the end.

AFTER TRAFALGAR.

And is he dead : is Nelson dead,
 The gentle and the brave ?
Has the sunlight of England's might
 Set in its ocean-grave ?

Yes, he is dead ! God spared him to us
 Until their flag was low,
Until our shore for evermore
 Was proof against the foe.

He came, as comes the rain in summer,
 To make the parch'd fields smile,
Or as a sail that wreck'd men hail
 Upon a desert isle.

He was a meteor sent from heaven
 To cross the tyrant's path
As a forecast, ere hope was past,
 Of overtaking wrath.

And, like a meteor, his passage
  Was brief as it was bright,
As if such glare we could not bear
  With feeble human sight.

He died, as died on Pisgah Moses,
  Just when his task was done,
As Moses too he might but view
  The guerdon he had won.

He passed, as erst had pass'd Elijah,
  'Mid thunder and 'mid fire,
When he had seen the evil queen
  Quail at the presage dire.

This to his country : but to me,
  His more and less than wife,
The sun that shone has set and gone,
  The summer left my life.

He was the dawn that fill'd my heaven,
  The star that lit my night,
The goodly tree that shaded me
  Against the fierce noon-light.

He was my king, my Alexander,
  My seaman Pericles,
And but for him my fame were dim
  And my cup thick with lees.

And what if he look'd on my beauty,
  And said these cheeks were fair ;
Or vow'd my kiss to him was bliss,
  And smooth'd each wayward hair.

Was not Aspasia's chiefest glory
  The love that some call'd sin ?
And Rosamond, was she less fond
  Than Eleanor the Queen ?

I would not have our love forgotten,
  Be it or crown or crime ;
If it were wrong, 'twas not less strong
  Than others' of old time,

Whose names are monuments to virtue,
  Griselda and Elaine,
With him who died at Juliet's side,
  And her of Allemaine.

But he is dead, and would to God
  That I were as they are
Whose deathlong sleep is in the deep
  Off stormy Trafalgar.

ON A NEWBORN BABE.

What is the secret of this bud
Of pink and simple babyhood,
That thrusts its head above the soil
Into this world of joy and toil?

We presage little of the shoot
Which rises from the hidden root,
But that leaf and stalk will follow
With the coming of the swallow.

And what its aftergrowth will be,
Whether flower or stately tree,
Only the Pow'r that made it knows;
We can but watch it as it grows.

And, noting each unfolded leaf
The bud detaches from its sheaf,
Call back those of trees and flowers
Which we knew in other hours,

Saying that sweet carnation
Had such a budding as this one,
And yon fair lily in its youth
Just such a soft-upspringing growth ;

Or that the pine, so tall and strong,
Grew in this wise when it was young,
And the oak that rules the wild wood
Was as this one in its childhood.

What will this bud be, sweet or strong,
As the years hasten it along?
Will it be delicate and fair,
Or rear its boughs into the air?

Will it be rifled of its bloom
To decorate a gilded room,
Or with broad trunk scorning danger
Flout the rising tempest's anger?

I would that this small bud you see
Just as a moss-rose bud should be,
As sweet to scent, as full of dew,
As beautiful in shape and hue ;

And as the lily, free from stain,
And fresh as hedgerows after rain,
And as the daisy, ever-blooming
Radiant and unpresuming.

I would that this small bud you see
Should grow into a linden tree,
Should put forth tender leaves in spring,
And after burst out blossoming ;

Should give in summer heat a shade
Beneath its leafy colonnade,
And each year send out new branches
In green fragrant avalanches.

And, if its fibre stouter be,
That it turn out a brave oak tree,
Late in the leaf, in increase slow,
But match for all the winds that blow,

Standing in green old age alone
When all its mates are dead and gone,
Type of constancy and greatness
Grander for its very lateness.

EST DEUS IN NOBIS.

I

I have that in me
That sooner, or in later years, will out ;
Idlesse may win me
To waste good hours—I may be clogg'd with doubt
Or cloy'd with pleasure ;
Or weary with a burthen of despair,
Or lull'd with leisure
To sleep ; or by unintermittent care
Hawk'd at and hunted ;
Or by the dead'ning round of daily toil
Worn thin and blunted ;
Or by the promise of a richer spoil,
My goal forgotten,
Used for a baser purpose ; or, with lust
And languor rotten,
Prove a dishonest guardian of my trust.

II.

The dam that hinders
The race shall burst, replenish'd by the rain ;
The smould'ring cinders,
Fann'd by the bellows, shall burst out again ;
The warworn charger,
Prick'd by the spur, shall cut through ringing foes ;
Young hope grown larger
Shall throttle old despair, and worst the woes :
The drowning swimmer
Shall tip the sand, and stagger to the shore ;
The lamp's low glimmer
Shall drink fresh oil, and mimic light once more ;
The weary spirit's
Weakness shall gather strength ; my brain shall prove
That it inherits
A legacy of thought for men to love.

JUVENILIA

THE LAST OF THE BRITONS, OR THE LEGEND OF DUNMAIL RAISE.

Round Grisedale's mountain-girdled mere
The latest moon of all the year
Lights in its wane an ancient host,
Each warrior an armour'd ghost,
Arm'd with the arms our country bore
E'er its first foeman touch'd its shore :
Of bronze their sword, of flint their spear,
Their leathern shield a hide of deer,
A British host, the last that held
The land, that all was theirs of eld.
    Ten hundred years scarce pass'd away
After that first great Easter-day
E'er not a Keltic lord was known
Through all the coasts of Albion,

Save in the stormy hills of Wales,
And Cornwall's mines, and Cumbria's dales,
    And Mona's citadel;
And Saxon was in league with Scot
From this his last and best lov'd lot
    The Briton to expel.
Then all at once the loyal men
Of Cymri leapt from rock and glen
    To join their king Dunmail;
From saddle-back'd Blencathra's height,
Where, hidden from the sun's good light,
    The tarn they call Bowscale
Reflects the stars at middle day,
While in its depths unfathom'd play
    That strange immortal twain,
The only fish in this wide earth
That liv'd at our Redeemer's birth :
    They know not death or pain,
But live until he comes again,
For they, they only, did remain
    Of that world-famous seven
Wherewith the 'Lord of Life' did feed
Those thousands four—this precious meed
    To them alone is given.
At once did Cumbria's noblest pour
From all the peaks of huge Skiddaw,
From Skiddaw's cub, since called Latrigg,
From Windermere and Newby Brig.

* High in the west from grim Sca'fell,
And wild Wastwater's lonely dell,
The dalesmen hurried down to bring
Arms, few but faithful to their king.
High in the east along that road,
The highest ever built, they strode :
And not a few from Langdale Pikes,
And Furness Fells and Furness Dykes,
    Which now the sea doth hold,
But flocks and beeves and giant trees,
And corn that shimmered in the breeze,
    Held in the days of old.
Ten thousand—good men all, and true—
Came where his royal standard flew,
    To fight for hearth and home ;
A home they'd held a thousand years
'Gainst Dane and Saxon, and the spears
    E'en of Imperial Rome.

    Hard by Helvellyn's mountain-steep,
Where Leathes' mere begins to peep,
Rises a knoll, in later days
Call'd in the dale King Dunmail's Raise.
Here 'neath the mountain's shoulders sheer
The road that runs from Windermere
Is one long hill from Grasmere shore
To Wy'burn town, six miles or more.
In such a pass three hundred men
Might drive ten thousand back again :

Upon this rise did Dunmail post
His faithful, but too scanty, host.
But what avails devotion high,
Or chivalrous fidelity,
When tenfold is the foeman's rank,
And pouring in on front and flank.
'Twas thus that royal Dunmail's might
Was shattered in that fatal fight ;
For while ten times ten-thousand men,
The Saxon host, charged up the glen,
Down huge Helvellyn's rugged side
Pour'd the fierce Scot as pours the tide
Of some long-prisoned mountain stream
When broken is th' opposing beam
That damm'd its flood and turn'd its flow
To drive the miller's wheel below ;
Or like the Cyclon blasts that sweep
Over the face of India's deep.
The Briton bravely met the charge
With levell'd spear and sturdy targe :
But vain—for, hemm'd on every hand,
Nought could avail the gallant band :
Not all the valour and the might
Of Arthur and each boasted knight
  Nam'd of the Table Round ;
Not all King Charlemagne's array
Of Paladins that on a day
  A grave with Roland found,

A fiercer charge—his host gives way,
And Scot and Saxon fierce to slay
Cut down the Britons man by man,
Till scarce a tithe of all the clan
Fight their way through to tell the tale
And save the crown of King Dunmail.
For he has lost his faithful brand,
And now is in the foeman's hand,
With both his sons, ill-fated three,
Doom'd to a conqueror's cruelty,
Their only crime that they did fight
To keep the realm that was their right.
Bound hand and foot with cords they lay
Until the ending of the fray
Should give their conqueror liberty
To revel in his cruel glee.
Then—such the custom of his day—
With his own hand does Edmond slay
The sire before the children's eyes
And blinds them soon as e'er he dies.

The Britons who escap'd the fray
Hid on the hills till close of day,
Then dug a grave twelve fathoms deep
And laid their monarch down to sleep,
And rais'd a cairn of boulders high
In homage to his memory :

Then wended in procession drear
To hide his crown in Grisedale mere.
With weapons fiercely clench'd they strode
Three miles along the Grasmere road,
Until they came to Grisedale barn,
And up the Faery glen did turn :
Awhile upon Seat-Sandal pause,
Then slowly wind through Grisedale Hause
Down to the mere and through the crown
Where Dollywaggon Pike sheers down.
Fierce was the wave and fierce the storm,
And mist-besieg'd the mountain's form ;
The Spirits of the Lake and hills
Were anger'd at their country's ills,
Anger'd that stranger-hands had ta'en
The Briton's last, best loved domain.
That night o'er forest, lake, and fell
Resounded many a ghostly yell ;
Around Helvellyn's giant man
With threat'ning glare the marsh-fire ran.
In becks, that yester summer's night
Scarce trickled down in shallows bright,
By deep and furious floods were borne
Great rifted rocks and trees uptorn :
The wind that scarce was heard at noon
Roar'd like an Indian typhoon,
And westward over Langdale Pikes
The breakers fell on Furness Dykes,

⁺And with one wild tremendous sweep
 Encompass'd in their greedy deep
 Tree, corn and cot, and grassy down
 From Lancaster to Barrow town.
 And by the forked fire from heaven
 The oldest Druid oak was riven.
 The oak-tree gods might reign no more
 Upon their native Britain's shore,
 But now must fly, to stay awhile
 In mother Mona's magic isle,
 And thence be driven in wild unrest
 For ever further, further west.
 Till, when five hundred years were gone,
 The land that tombs the setting sun
 Should feel the conquering foot of Spain ;
 Then, ousted from their home again
 With other byegone godheads lie
 In Limbo to eternity.

  The Britons ere the day was light
 Scal'd the o'erhanging mountain-height,
 And climbing, just as dawn began,
 Held council on Helvellyn Man.
 Full little did they deem that night
 That ev'ry eve, ere dawn was bright,
 Their souls must go to Dunmail's cairn
 And through the glen to Grisedale tarn ;

Then over Dollywaggon seek
The high Helvellyn's highest peak.
Yet so it is—for there are souls
Whom some almighty hand controls
To haunt some too-eventful scene,
Where in their lifetime they have been ;
Nor ever rest within their tomb
Until they have fulfill'd their doom:
The souls of all who've follow'd Cain,
The souls of all by murder slain,
Until the murderer pay the due
For him that fell and him that slew ;
The soul of him whose life was ill,
Who perish'd unrepentant still,
And him who treasure has conceal'd,
Until his treasure be reveal'd.
And so it is that Dunmail's host
Still haunt the battle-field in ghost.
Did they but deign betray their trust
Their souls might rest in hallow'd dust,
But while they guard their monarch's crown
May never to their tomb go down.
And so each day from fall of night
Until the morrow-morn is bright,
Through Grisedale pass that ghostly clan
March grimly to Helvellyn Man.
And ev'ry night from Grisedale tarn
They bring a stone to Dunmail's cairn,

*To show their sovereign that still
They're faithful to his royal will :
And when the cairn doth reach as high
As Dunmail 'neath the earth doth lie,
Once more shall be his flag unfurl'd
For the great Battle of the World,
For that great battle that must be
Before the day of Equity ;
When ev'ry man shall have his own
Each proud usurper overthrown,
When Israel shall reign once more
Upon the promised country's shore,
And Cossack, Georgian, and Pole
Be freed from Muscovite control.
Then Dummail with his British spears
Again shall sally from the meres,
And free his own, his native land
From Saxon, Dane, and Norman hand.
From southmost Cornwall to Carlisle,
From Mona to the Kentish Isle
The Cymri, as in days of yore,
Shall rule our land from shore to shore ;
And all the Cymri clans bow down
Before the might of Dunmail's crown ;
The crown that erst in Grisedale's deep
His trusty host did nightly keep,
Now, after many a hundred years,
Again upon his head appears.

But never shall appear again
The gods that ruled our island then ;
Their day is past, their oaks are fell'd
In which their ritual was held.
No other gods shall be adored
Through all the earth but Judah's Lord,
And they be in that lifeless spot
For ever and for aye forgot.

But though that British army range
Each midnight on that journey strange,
No eye can see their forms, no ear
Their footfall or their voices hear,
Save on one night—upon that night
When dies away the waning light
Of the last moon of all the year :
Then if thou stand by Grisedale mere,
Betwixt the midnight hour and dawn,
When spirits move and graveyards yawn,
Through Grisedale Hause to Grisedale tide
Thou'lt see a ghostly army glide
In Keltic harness—such a host
Fought the first Roman on our coast.
See thou provoke them not to strife,
'Twere likeliest to cost thy life.
But should'st thou venture to accost
By Father, Son, and Holy Ghost,

And bid them show thee where the crown
In Grisedale mere lies low a-down,
They needs must show thee ; and if then
Thou take the crown, they ne'er again
Shall leave their grave for Grisedale tarn,
Nor Dunmail ever leave his cairn ;
But other kings shall free the land
From Saxon, Dane, and Norman hand.
So, if thou see that spirit host,
In pity do not thou accost,
Nor to indulge an idle whim
Or caitiff greed do harm to him ;
But gaze with awe and tell the tale
Of that weird army of Dunmail.

ROMAN CIRENCESTER.

I.

Only a battlement of turfen green !
　　Only a footworn floor of alien stone !
Yet guarded by that turf how oft hath been
　　Proctor and Emperor in days agone !
　　Over these hills have Roman eagles flown
　　And dy'd them Tyrian with native blood ;
　　On this worn stone sweet Roman maidens trod,
Or British captives dragg'd by Roman captors strode.,

II.

Oh ! oftentimes on sweltering summer day,
　　When haply fallen in a reverie
Beneath a leafy canopy I lay,
　　Or shadow'd by a beetling rockery,
　　Hath fancy carried me to days gone by
　　When huge primeval forests cloth'd the land,
　　And yet untouch'd by man's presumptuous hand
All was, as Heaven had made it, natural and grand.

III.

High on the hills in woods of uncut pine
   The royal stag the juicy herbage brows'd ;
'Neath the broad oaks the eburn-tusked swine
   Now revell'd in an acorn feast, now drows'd
   Fearless of ill, unhunted and unrous'd :
   Above, the wild bees stor'd their honey, press'd
   From myriad wild flower blossoms, in a nest
Scoop'd in the antique trees by which the swine did
   rest.

IV.

The kine uncall'd came to the milcher's hand,
   Shedding of creamy wealth ungrudging store ;
The corn, unsown, sprung from unfurrow'd land,
   Corn such as Egypt's galleys never bore
   To Rome's imperial quays in days of yore :
   The trees ungraff'd with such rare fruitage bent
   As Picus and Vertumnus never sent
For gifts to coy Pomone when they a-wooing went.

V.

Anon the woaded Briton slew the boar
   That wander'd in the forest, and the hart
That lorded on the mountain ; then no more
   Did bounteous nature unearn'd wealth impart ;
   No more did wild bees in the hollow heart

Of age-worn oak garner a honey hoard
For man to plunder, nor the kine afford
Their milky store untended : no, nor the generous
    sward

VI.

Shoot forth its crops unseeded : then the trees,
    That erst had been so fruitful, died away ;
And that fair fruit, with which the western breeze,
    And Phoebus' beams, what time he woke the day,
    Kissing its cheeks, most lovingly did play,
    No longer was engendered, but mean sloes,
    And nurtureless wild raspberries, and those
That grow upon the bramble, the hawthorn, and wild
    rose.

VII.

These were the Briton's food, these and the beasts
    Stricken by sling or cudgel in the chace ;
The only draught that mingled in his feasts
    Poor unfermented mead ; his resting place
    A hovel in the forest, or crevasse
    Cleft by some earth-upheaval or ice-tide ;
    His only garb a cloke of untanned hide,
Undeck'd, save by the blue with which his limbs
    were dy'd.

VIII.

Such was the earliest lord, ye Cotteswolds,
   That o'er your woody summits used to fare ;
And where, anon, were cornfields and sheepfolds,
    With half-tamed hounds he'd course the timorous
      hare,
    Or hand to hand grapple the mountain bear :
    His only craft and knowledge, hunting lore ;
    His only trade and chiefest calling, war ;
His only joy, to quaff his mead, the struggle o'er.

IX.

But who are these that scale the Cotteswold ?
   What military pageant ?   What great clan,
So many, and so mighty, and so bold ?
    Seest not the eagles glist'ning in the van ?
    'Tis Corus with his Romans : the Belgian
    Cowers before their thund'rous clarion blare ;
    The Atrebate shrinks to his forest lair
In nerveless dread, or fighting falls in fierce despair.

X.

Feast on, sleep on in peace, thou grizzly boar !
   Stalk on, old stag ! no hunter comes to day ;
Store on, wild bees ! no hand shall rob your store ;
    Thou timorous hare, have out thy fearless play ;
    To day the bear uncheck'd may rend his prey ;

No coracle shall leave the river side,
  No fibre-nets shall sweep the Severn tide,
Its waters with no spear-struck otter's blood be
  dy'd.

XI.

What change is this upon the Cotteswolds?
  Where erst were virgin forests of grim pine,
Of beasts, wild birds, and hunting men the holds,
    Rich corncrofts teem with grain and fruit trees
      shine,
    Gemmed, as it were, with fruitage nectarine;
    The harmless swine wallow where once the boar;
    The milch-goats skip where strode the stag of
      yore;
The shy kine graze the hills, and fear the bear no
  more.

XII.

Here Corus built Corinium, whose walls
  Were doomed to last for twice a thousand years!
Soon, where had been mud hovels, rose great halls
    Of porphyry and marble; 'mid the breres
    Peeped villas, such as nestle by the piers
    Of Tiber and Benactus, lightly made
    With hanging eave and pillared colonnade,
Against tempestuous rain or angry sun a shade.

XIII.

In such arcade did Flaccus on a day
  Woo poor fair Cinara ; in such a home
Catullus sang his ditties, or at play
  With lovely, wanton Lesbia, did roam ;
  To such a porch did graceful Julia come
  As Manlius' bride ; amid such luxury
  Of cultured flowers and native greenery
Old Maro sued the nymphs in pastoral melody.

XIV.

Adown by bank of tributary Churn
  Rose the great baths, the baths where most of all
The Roman loved to linger, were it morn,
  Mid-day, or afternoon, or evenfall,
  Plashing a soothing water-madrigal,
  A fitting lullaby to such a leisure :
  Or cunning minstrels lured back truant pleasure
With Amphionic strains in old Œolian measure.

XV.

Westward, a little south, behold a stade,
  Turf-velveted (such velvet did appear
In Tempe, or an intermittent glade
  Of Dian's Latmian forest) : tier on tier
  Rows of onlooking benches did uprear,

Hewn on the mountain-shoulder ; hence the
    face
Of stoled maiden peered upon the space,
While in their furious course huge chariots drave
    apace !

XVI.

The pageant changes—man with man doth vie ;
    Both Titans, captive children of the North,
Bred in the warrior-craft of Italy,
      To sate their captor's blood-lust : come they
      forth
      In pride of strength and manhood, all a-wrath,
      To battle for their lives and other's play.
      Olympians, where were ye on that day,
To see such goodly blood so lightly poured away?

XVII.

In deadly feud they grapple—one doth fall ;
    Oozes the ruddy life-blood from a wound :
Gleams at his throat the falchion : hear him call
      For mercy !   In the galleries around
      Do maids and fellow-Britons hear the sound.
      Can maidens see, unmoved, such agony ?
      Or hearkening, not pity such a cry ?
Will British heroes see a stricken brother die ?

XVIII.

Thumbs deadly down !   The unpitied hero dies !
  Mad crowd, is death so lovely, of such worth
That ye must make him such rich sacrifice ?
  Degenerate Briton, traitor to thy birth,
  Better hadst thou lain dead in mother-earth,
  Or crouch'd in perilous forest-wild forlorn !
  Ungentle maid, better wert thou unborn
Than this so piteous prayer with such unpity scorn.

XIX.

'Tis over : maid and Briton both lie dead ;
  The galleries with weeds are overgrown :
Charger and car alike are perished !
  From the void ring comes no beseeching moan
  Of sorely-stricken warrior overthrown !
  The stately bath has gone ; no plash is heard
  Save haply of a startled water-bird,
Or sheeny snake by foot of passing traveller stirred.

XX.

Gone are the pleasant villas on the hill ;
  Gone the great marble temples of the vale ;
Never again hear we the lute's sweet trill,
  Or noisy ring of legionary mail !
  All, all are gone, and live not but in tale ;
  Saving a turfen rampart on the moor,
  Low, ruinous wall, or worn mosaic floor,
Sole trace of that great race that ruled our land of yore.

THE BATTLE OF FIRE AND WATER.

A PARAPHRASE FROM HOMER, ILIAD XXI.

I.

Scamander, king of every Asian river,
The sentinel of Priam's sovranty,
Where'er he spied Achilles there did ever
See Ilium's noblest stark and stricken lie :
So he, to aid them in their misery,
Marshalled his seething eddies to the fight,
And forward charged with all his watery might,
If he on Peleus' son might chance to wreak his spite.

II.

So Xanthus led his billow troop, bedewing
His either bank with showers of foamy spray ;
Meanwhile, hard by, great Peleus' son was hewing
Through Ilium's staggered ranks a mortal way ;
Down fell the heroes, as on that dread day
When Earth's gigantic brood their flag unfurled
'Gainst Chronos' son, and he their myriads hurled
In thunder-stricken panic on the infant world.

III.

He paused, and of a sudden saw Scamander,—
That scarce a minute since had wandered by
As listlessly as kine at pasture wander,—
Spurring a grey-maned breaker, roaring high,
As when a steed, hearing the battle cry,
Pricks his keen ears, and, e'en before the goad,
Flies to the charge.   Achilles knew his bode,
And half bold, half in fear, to meet the river strode.

IV.

Nor strode he far : they met, and straight the billow
Swept the loud-vaunting chieftain from his feet,
And there had overwhelmed him ; but a willow,
A bowed, gnarled willow, stayed the river fleet,
While he to Hera raised his sad entreat.
Meanwhile, Scamander, victor in the fray,
Chafed at the check, and loath to lose his prey,
Uptore the tree and down-stream swept them both
    away.

V.

'O Hera, lady Hera, white-armed goddess Hera,
Vouchsafe thine ear to this my piteous plaint ;
The river rolls his billow squadrons nearer.
    The tree is old, and I am passing faint ;
    O goddess pitying hear and set a straint

On eddying Scamander.'   Hera heard
Achilles' prayer, and straight Hephaestus stirred
(Her son, the God of Fire) with bitter gibe and word.

VI.

O son, thou clubfoot Suzerain of Fire,
　　With thee again Scamander thinks to vie,
And reckless of thy wrath and blazing ire,
　　Doth thee again to battle-royal defy,
　　And Peleus' son with impious wave doth ply :
　　Blaze forth, and make the braggart stream repent,
　　Nor cease to wreak thy furious intent—
Howe'er he crave thee grace—till I do nod assent.'

VII.

So Hera spake, the white-armed Queen : to sate
　　her,
　　Her son, Hephaestus, fanned his fiery breath,
And in his forge deep down in Ætna's crater
　　Drew his firebrand from its volcanic sheath.
　　Then all around went ruin and black death :
　　Where'er his parching indignation fell
　　He scorched the pleasant meads of asphodel—
The meads where most of all Scamander loved to
　　dwell.

VIII.

Scamander, all too ready for the battle,
  Hurls his great rampant billows on the foe,
And where the greedy flames the loudest rattle
  There most his water-javelins doth throw.
  Hephaestus rises stronger from each blow,
  As that old hydra, by Alcides slain,
  From every wound another head did gain,
And from the very steel fresh vigour did attain.

IX.

Thus Clubfoot beat Scamander, whose poor waters
  Seethed o'er the banks in powerless agony ;
And all the water-nymphs, Scamander's daughters,
  In haste Hephaestus' fiery breath to flee,
  Fled to their father's father, the wide sea ;
  The great brown eels turned on their backs and
    died,
  The wolf-fish writhed and wrung his thorny side,
And not one breath of life was left in Xanthus tide.

X.

Then Xanthus thus bespake the Lord of Fire :
  ' Hephaestus, we were playmates years ago,
And thine was my, and mine was thy, desire ;
  But now thou scath'st me with thy murtherous glow.
  Am I, then, Troy's best friend, or thy worst foe?

Spare me : be thine the palm of victory.'
Hephaestus hearkened not unto his cry,
But still with wrath unminished did his waters ply.

XI.

Then Xanthus cried to Hera, Queen of Heaven :
  ' Hear me, O Queen, and bid the Clubfoot
    cease.
My waters seethe ; my banks with heat are riven—
  My pleasant banks where in the times of peace,
  Ere harmless Troy became the bait of Greece,
  The Trojan swains and Trojan maidens strolled,
  And that old tale these listed and those told—
The tale that lasts for ever learnt in the age of gold.

XII.

' But now thy son, Hephaestus, in his anger
  Hath scorched my banks, and all my children
    slain :
Why should I seek of Troy and Trojan danger ?
  If thou wilt bid thy son his wrath restrain,
  I swear in sooth that I will ne'er again
  A Durdan aid against a Danaan foe,
  Nor cross Achilles in his work of woe,
E'en though high Troy itself with Grecian fire should
  glow.'

XIII.

So Xanthus prayed ; and Hera heard his prayer,
    And nodded to her son. At her command
He sent his flames to their Ætnean lair,
    And from his mortal work withheld his hand,
    And in volcanic scabbard sheathed his brand.
    Scamander flowed 'mid death on either shore :
    Achilles smote more hotly than before,
Nor was he braved again through those ten years of
    war.

ST. PAUL AT ATHENS.

I.

In Athens fair (who knows not Athens fair,
   The grandest city of Hellenic story?)
Stood Paul, 'mid temples towering in the air,
   Built in the brightest blaze of Attic glory.
The splendours that the Parthenon surrounded
       His eyes did greet ;
And Athens' self, by ancient Cecrops founded,
       Lay at his feet.

II.

Hard by, Cephissus rolled his silver tide ;
   Hard by, his rival, rippled fleet Ilissus :
Fragrant and fair, fringing the river-side,
   Grew lily-white and golden-eyed Narcissus :
Nodded their fruitful plumes on Lycabettus
       Fat olive trees :
With murmurous hum on flowery Hymettus
       Plundered the bees.

III.

High in the city of the violet crown
   Altars sent up their incense-breath to Pallas ;
Shrines rich with gifts from many a conquered town
   Rose there to all the myriad gods of Hellas.
Unshrined, unincensed, and undecorated,
        Giftless, alone,
Arose a lowly altar, dedicated
        ' To the Unknown.'

IV.

On that wide sea of Pagan pageantry,
   On fretted capitals and braded bases,
On pinnacles that sprung to meet the sky,
   On fairest forms of goddesses and graces,
He careless glanced ; but meantime haply lighting
        On the poor stone
Of that low altar, read the mystic writing,
        ' To the Unknown.'

V.

He climbed the terraced slope of Ares' hill,
   The hill oft trodden by that grand old heathen,
' The wisest man that knew not God ; ' and still
   The echoes of his wisdom lingered, wreathen

P

Round every stone :—but now a wiser and greater
    That terrace trod,
Who told not of the creature but Creator,
    Who told of God.

VI.

' My brothers, Men of Athens, that Unknown
    Whom ye do honour by the altar graven
With that strange title, he is God alone
    Of all the gods : he made the earth and heaven
And all that therein are ; he is the giver
    Of life and light ;
From everlasting he hath lived, and ever
    Lives infinite.

VII.

' We are his children ; in the days of old
    We were like him, pure, sorrowless, unsinning,
Till our first parent by his error sold
    The birthright of our lineage, thereby winning
Eternal sorrow and toil, had not the kindness
    Of Christ, God's Son,
Undone with his own blood whate'er in blindness
    Our sire had done.

VIII.

' Christ's joy was not in temples built by men,
    Or choicest limnings from Apelles' easel
Or sweetest strains from Sophoclean pen,
    Or statues called to life by Phidias' chisel ;

Beauty and grace, by Athens' sons so prized,
> To him were nought ;
The poor, the halt, the erring, the despised
> Were what he sought.'

IX.

Thus he : meanwhile in wonderment the men
> Learnt the first measures of that sweet old story
Of him who died for us and rose again
> To sit at God's right hand in heaven in glory.
He ceased : straight some with jeers his words rejected,
> And some received
But doubtingly ; some questioned, some neglected,
> Some few believed.

X.

Hail Dionysius, Areopagite,
> First Attic thou to drink the living waters;
Sweet Damaris, hail, thou first to see the light
> Of all Athena's hundred-hundred daughters :
Hail faithful few, sagest of Attic sages,
> The first who trod
The path of Life writ in the sacred pages,
> The path to God.

VERGIL'S TENTH ECLOGUE.

Grant me this latest boon, sweet Arethusa,
To Gallus let me sing a little ditty,
Such ditty as Lycoris' self might hearken.
Who'd grudge a song to Gallus?   Grant this ditty
So never may the bitter Dorian water
Mingle her flood with thine, what time thou glidest
Under the waves to the Sicilian island.
Sing! let us tell the hapless love of Gallus,
While comely goats the tender herbage nibble.
We sing not to deaf ears; the whispering forests
Will give us back our every word in answer.
'What glades, what forests held you, river maidens,
While Gallus pined with love all ill-requited?
'Twas not Parnassus' crest; it was not Pindus,
Not Aganippe on the Arnan mountain,
That held you back that day.   The very laurels,
The very tamarisks shed tears for Gallus,
While Gallus lay beneath that rock deserted :
Pine-bearing Maenalus and frore Lycaeus
Shed tears for him.
                    See ! here the sheep are standing ;

The sheep tire not of us, god-gifted poet ;
See that thou never weary of thy herding :
Adonis' self shed tears beside a river,
Comely Adonis.   See ! here comes the shepherd,
Here come the ploughmen lagging, and Menaleas,
Wet from his sodden winter acorn-harvest,
All ask thee ' Whence this love ? ' Here comes Apollo.
' Gallus, art mad ? know that thy sweet Lycoris,
Through snow and war, another love hath followed.'
Here comes Silvanus, crowned with country beauty,
Waving great lily flowers and blooming fennel,
And Pan, the God of Arcady, oft ruddied
With blood of elderberry or vermilion.
Quoth he, ' Will't cease ? Love values not such service.
The meadows never weary of the moisture,
The wild bees never weary of the clover,
The she goat never wearies of the pasture,
Nor Love of tears.'   Then Gallus, all too-mournful,
' It must be : nathless, Arcads, sing your ditty
To your own hills : ye only, happy Arcads,
Are great in song.   So might I rest in quiet,
If, when I died, your pipes might tell my story.
Would I had been one of your country fellows,
Herd of your sheep, or dresser of your vintage !
Were Phyllis then my darling, or Amyntas,
Or what love else,—what if thou'rt dark, Amyntas ?
Dark are the violets and hyacinth blossoms—
With me in willow arbours should they rest them

'Mid trailing vines, Phyllis should pick me flowers,
Amyntas warble me a country ditty.

' Lycoris, here are woods, cool springs, soft meadows,
Oh ! might I here with thee live out my life-time !
Me the mad love of battle keeps a-warring,
Compassed by darts, and face to face with foemen.
Thou far from home—oh ! might I doubt such
     story !—
Hard-heart, without me and alone, beholdest
The frozen floods of Rhine and Alpine snowdrifts.
Ah ! may no frosts hurt thee ! no sharp ice-splinters
Maim thy soft feet ! Now will I go and warble,
To the rude tune of a Sicilian shepherd,
The songs I made me in Chalcidian measure.'
' I fain would suffer pain, if I must suffer,
Amid the haunts of beasts, or in the forests,
And on the bark of young trees stamp my passion.
The trees will grow, and with them grow my passion ;
Meantime with nymphs on Maenalus I'll clamber,
Or hunt the high-souled boar : no frosts shall keep me
From compassing with hounds the Arcad passes.
Methinks, I go by cliffs and whispering forests,
And shoot from Parthian bow the shafts of Cydon ;
As if this were a simple for my passion,
Or that unkindly god would learn him kindness
From ills of men.   Never again the oak-nymphs,
Nor e'en my ditties please me.   O my forests
Once more farewell ! My troubles cannot move him,

E'en if amid the ice I drink of Hebrus,
And stand the snow of wet Sithonian winter;
E'en if, what time the hearts of lofty elm-trees
Wither with heat and die, beneath the crab star
In Æthiopy I ply a shepherd's calling,
Love conquers, all to love would I surrender.'
  'Ye goddesses of the Pierian fountain,
This shall suffice your poet to have warbled,
Sitting and weaving rushes into baskets.
Slight as it is you'll do a boon to Gallus,
Gallus, the friend for whom my love grows hourly,
As fast as shoot green alders in the spring-time.
Now rise, for shade is hurtful to the singer,
The shade of junipers is ever hurtful;
The shade is even hurtful to the harvest.
Go home content, my goats, go, night is falling.'

THE LAST OF THE VIKINGS.

The day had sprung : red rose the autumn sun ;
A sweet September morning had begun—
And ne'er rose autumn sun on scene more fair
Than on the Yorkshire river winding there.
Yestre'en its banks were desolate and still,
Save for the otter's plunge, and throstle's trill,
Nor aught of human handiwork might seem,
Save the old wooden bridge that spanned the stream ;
To-day its banks are strewn with many a tent
Of outland men, and uncouth armament ;
To-day upon the breezes bellies forth
The black marauder Raven of the North ;
To-day's sun rises on the dreadest host
That since Canute's has landed on our coast.
But all is still as ever it has been—
No murmur mars the softness of the scene ;
The sea-kings slumber full as peacefully
As children in their careless infancy.
    At length they wake : No need of arms to-day
To meet a Saxon foe in war array.
To-day is one of triumph and delight,
Reaping the harvest of a well-fought fight.

To-day must England's noblest yielded be,
As pledges of her subject fealty :
Scarboro' is burnt, and many a town to burn,
The Northmen victors whereso'er they turn ;
The brother earls, with all their earldom's might,
At Fulford gate routed and put to flight ;
And York herself by cravens to the foe
Yielded before she took or gave a blow.

    Therefore, to-day no arms the Northmen bear,
But weeds of peace, and mien of triumph wear,
And gaze toward the distant town to see
The hostages of England's fealty.

    But what is this that glitters in the sun ?
What hides the dust, so thickly rolling on ?
What clash is this upon the breezes borne ?
What flash of metal in the glimmering morn ?
The clash is that of sword, and shield, and spear,
The flash, of coat of mail, and burnished gear.
The hostages are many, and their plight
Not of men come to yield, but come to fight.

    Then Tostig rose and laced his helmet on,
And thus spake he to Harold Sigurdsson :

    ' Arm, son of Sigurd, arm thee for the fray ;
The baby-earls keep not their troth to-day ;
These are no hostages of England's faith ;
Their bode is not of homage, but of death ;
The Southern thegns are mingled with the North ;
The strength of Saxon England has come forth ;

Thingman and Churl, Angle and Man of Kent,
Are ranged together in yon armament.
Seest thou those banners blazing in the van,
The Golden Dragon, and the Fighting Man?
These go not forth but where my brother goes,
Twin heralds of destruction to his foes.
Turn, arm your host as soon as e'er you can ;
To fight Earl Harold is to fight a man :
No boy-earl he to fly before thy charge,
Ere yet thy sword-point clatter on his targe,
But used to dash his axe into the mail
As in the yielding snowdrift sinks the hail.'

Then answered Sigurd's Harold, wrathfully :
'No man on earth hath ever made me flee,
Not when I warred on many a doubtful day
With the fierce swarms of sunburnt Africa ;
Not when the bold Varangians stood alone
Against the banded might of Cæsar's throne ;
Nor in the thousand fights by land and sea,
Here, in the North, for my supremacy—
The thousand fights fought on the stormy main
With Swedish Berserker, and Viking Dane.
And shall the Sea King turn his back in flight
From men already worsted in the fight ?
Perish the thought !   The man who lacks a shield
Has one hand more his deadlier sword to wield.'

So spake the King, and bade his men advance
The famous wall of serried shield and lance.

Meanwhile the Saxon, turning to his host,
With valiant words their valour did accost :
  ' O ye stouthearted Saxons, who have wrought
Deeds of renown on fields where Ironside fought ;
O conquerors of many a stubborn fray,
Where Athelstan and Alfred led the way ;
To-day ye battle with an enemy
Dreader than ever Alfred did defy.
  ' Ye sturdy Danes, who won you your repute
Behind the conquering banners of Canute ;
Ye conquerors of many a stubborn fray—
Where Berserker and Viking barred the way—
To-day ye battle with an enemy
Dreader than ever Canute did defy.
  ' Great hearts of England, Angles ye and Danes,
Earls of the North, and stout West Saxon thegns,
By every memory of each fiercest field,
Where none of you would to the others yield,
Whether ye fought for Edmund or Canute,
The foe ye front is worthy your repute.
Think ye, old Danes, when sounds the bugle ' On '
Of those dear English homes your blood has won.
Think ye, young Saxons, when ye bare your blades,
Of your fair heritage and blue-eyed maids.
Saxon and Jute, East Anglian and Dane,
In battle fierce contest ye once again,
Not now yourselves against yourselves to fight,
Ye worst each other in the foes ye smite ;

Whoe'er of you most foes shall overcome
They shall be hail'd as conquerors at home.
With Dane and Saxon fighting side by side
The whole wide hostile world might be defied ;
If ye but do to-day as ye have wrought
When Dane and Saxon with each other fought,
Never I wot shall Norway's Raven more
Feast on our fair united England's shore.

  'Great hearts of England, forward to the fray ;
Axes strike home, where Harold leads the way.'
  So spake the King, and both with shoutings loud
Their confidence and unity avowed.
But Harold, ere the battle had begun,
Saw Tostig's 'Lion' glitter in the sun,
And forward rode to where it rose display'd,
And to the escort of the banner said,—

  'If Tostig, son of Godwin, should be here,
I have a matter for his private ear.'
And straightway from the thickest of the crowd
Rode the proud earl, and cried in scorn and loud,

  'What man would speak with Tostig Godwinsson ?'
Then answer'd he : 'Earl Tostig, be it known
That from thy brother Harold am I come
To give thee greeting fair, and welcome home.
Then Tostig ask'd again, 'What gift is mine,
If I this gain and glory should resign ?
My fair broad earldom is another's now,
What shall be mine if I allegiance vow ?'

He answer'd : 'Thine old earldom shalt thou have,
Thy fair broad earldom by the northern wave ;
Or, if Northumbria irk to have thee back,
Of lands and living shalt thou have no lack,
For Gurth shall give his earldom unto thee
If thou return unto thy fealty.'

Then Tostig ask'd once more : 'What shall be done
For my ally, King Harold Sigurdsson ?'

He answer'd, half in anger half in mirth,
'Seven feet of grave in our good English earth ;
Or, seeing he is taller than his kin,
As much more as he need to lay him in.'

Then Tostig, son of Godwin, scornfully :
'How thinks my brother Harold this may be?
That I to battle in my cause should bring
Across the stormy main a mighty king,
And many a chief from many a northern coast,
And many a bold Berserker, tempest-tost ;
And when in fear you render to my might
The due ye would not render to my right,
Betray my friends and battle for my foes,
And pay my brother-chieftains back in blows?
My allies' foes are mine ; whate'er reward
Earl Tostig wins, he wins it with his sword.'
So spake the son of Godwin in reply.

Whereat King Harold rode back mournfully ;
While gazing on the Saxon, wondering,
Thus to Earl Tostig spake the northern king :

'Who was the Saxon lord that spake with thee?
In sooth no giant in respect of me,
But yet methought he bore him royally.'
    Then to him spake Earl Tostig, answering :
' My brother Harold Godwinsson, O king.'
    Then Sigurd's Harold wrathfully replied :
' Why spak'st thou not?   So surely had he died.'
    Then Tostig thought him of the days agone,
Of happy boyish hours for ever flown,
When he and Harold ranged the forest wide,
Or climbed in contest up the mountain side ;
Of generous strife within their father's hall,
Of many a well-boxed bout and wrestled fall,
And, mad with hate and injury and ill,
Proved him a soldier and a Saxon still ;
So answered he the Northman haughtily :
' To murder any man be far from me
Who comes to parley, trusting in my faith ;
But 'twere, indeed, dishonour worse than death
To murder my own brother, here to give
Life and broad fair domains on which to live.'

    The Saxon bugle sounded to the charge ;
The Northman formed his wall of spear and targe—
The stout shield-wall that broke the foeman's might,
And ever came victorious from the fight.
The horsemen charge in vain ; the shields are firm
As granite cliffs against an ocean storm ;

The spears are merciless as reefs of rock
To shipwrecked Dragons shivering with the shock.
The Saxon horse shrunk backward, as the sea
Bounds baffled from the harbour masonry :
Thrice charged and failed they ; thrice unmoved the
    North
With serried shield and spear defied their wrath ;
But, when the Saxons charged and failed again,
No longer could their eagerness contain,
But broke their ranks, and fell upon the foe
Like toppling cliffs upon the sea below.
The Saxons fled as spray before the blast ;
The North drove on them furious and fast.
But, see ! they rally ; see ! the Northmen fly,
And those who fled rush back to victory :
'Tis Harold and his thingmen—in a wedge
With axes fenced along its triple edge.
Is any struck—no need to strike again ;
Where English axes fall, there lie the slain.
Vikings, till now unused to fail or fly,
Flee in dismay, or, failing flight, must die.
Just as a bank that many a year defies
The fiercest storms that from the ocean rise,
Though with its fall it irresistibly
Beats down the assailing forces of the sea,
Yet fallen melts away before the tide
Of that whose fiercest storm it erst defied ;

Much like that tide upon the fallen earth
Swept Harold's axes on the shattered North.
But, see ! they rally in their turn—what form
Is this that looms so huge against the storm,
As, when the sea dashes the earth away,
Stands out a rock that hidden in it lay?
What man is this so glorious and so great
That leads the Northmen back to face their fate?
'Tis Sigurd's son : he strides before his bands
Wielding his greedy blade with both his hands ;
And, as he bears upon the hostile throng,
Chaunting in god-like voice his battle-song :

    ' Last night I dreamed a dream, and seemed to be
In Norway, by the borders of the sea ;
And all my ships lay ranged on either hand
Waiting the sign to launch them from the land,
Long Serpents fifteen score ; but on the stern
Of each sat brooding a black baleful erne :
While overhead, with trough and pitchfork bare,
A wild Witch Wife rode screaming through the air.
Then I awoke all trembling, I who ne'er,
Since I had known of aught, had known a fear.

    ' And then I slept again, and dreamt I stood
Here in this England, by the northern flood.
Behind, arrayed for battle, stood my men,
Of chosen brave three bands of thousands ten.
Before, advanced the army of the land,
The Saxon axe against the Northman brand.

I looked again : in front of them there strode
A huge witchwife, who on a Were Wolf rode ;
And, in her hand a pitchfork, fell upon
The bravest of my following, one by one,
And thrust them down the wolf's gigantic jaw,
Till all that followed me were in his maw.
And then I woke, trembling with fear once more,
Twice fearful now, who never feared before.
But what care I for vision or for dream ?
Those who are doomed to die, must die, I deem :
And where so glorious for a man to die
As battle, be it rout or victory ?
Forward, ye sons of Odin, win or lose,
They only perish whom the Valkyrs choose !
And those the Valkyrs choose, I ween, must fall,
Though warded in by warrior and wall.'

Chaunting this lay, he dashed upon the foe ;
Nor slow the Northmen, where he went, to go.
Saxon and Dane before the giant yield,
As from the Dragons' bows the salt-sea field.
Saxon and Dane before his arm go down,
As when in August fields the corn is mown.
Where'er he comes, those shrink in terror back ;
Where'er he goes, these follow to attack.
But who is this ?   See, full before his path.
A single warrior defies his wrath.
Lordly his mien—who is this venturous lord
That dares defy the might of Harold's sword ?

'Tis English Harold—battle-axe in hand
He waits the onset of the Northman's brand.
Down shore the deadly blade : the shivered shield
Fell in two 'fenceless fragments on the field.
But ere the king, recovered from the force
Of his own blow, could hasten on his course,
The Saxon dealt a blow upon his helm
That well-nigh won him, then and there, his realm ;
The Northman staggered—ne'er had he, I trow,
Felt such a manly buffet on his brow—
Then tossed his helm aside, and onward drave
To dash his daring foeman to the grave.
Swung is the brand again—upon the field,
Unhappy Harold, lies thy faithless shield.
What shall avail to fence the deadly blow ?
But Harold, eyeing steadfastly the foe,
Stood to his ground, with balanced axe prepared
To give a blow, or given blow to ward :
Poised is his England's future in the air ;
Who conquers here conquers a kingdom fair.
An arrow whistles—in Hardrada's throat
Is heard the deadly, gurgling, final note.
　　The Saxons charge : the Northmen, wavering,
Stand round the fallen body of their king.
' Forward ! ' cries Harold : straight the Northmen
　　　yield,
And fly before the Saxons from the field.
The victors follow close, and now they stand

Hard by the Raven Waster of the Land ;
And even now it were in Harold's hand,
When sudden 'twixt the standard and the king—
Known by his armour's golden shimmering—
Starts up the recreant Tostig, and defies
The bravest Saxon there to grasp the prize.
Yet Harold struck him not, but turned away
To where the Northmen still prolonged the fray,
Before the wooden bridge, which they must keep
If they would safely pass the Derwent's deep.
Upon this bridge a single Viking stood,
With dinted shield and red with alien blood :
Full forty men had fallen by the brand,
Which, yet untired, he wielded in his hand.
Then Harold, hailing, bade him yield his sword,
And lands and living should be his reward.
' No brave, or friend or foe, deserves to die ;
To yield with honour is a victory.'
The brave, unheeding, perished at his post—
He won Valhalla as his life he lost.

The bridge is ta'en—Earl Tostig dead—the North
But feebly combating the Saxon's wrath ;
Faint are their hopes—when sudden in their rear
The long-expected aid they see appear.
Are not their allies from the ships at length
Come in full armour and in all their strength ?
Is not this Eystein Orre, a warrior tried,
And soon to make his monarch's child his bride?

His bride, did fate permit; but, Eystein Orre,
Thy promised fair shall never greet thee more;
Thy bride shall be a chooser of the slain,
Or Harold's war-axe wedded to thy brain.
    Fierce were his troops for fight, but sore dis-
        tressed
With heat and haste, and by their armour pressed :
The Saxons too were wearied with the fray,
Faint with the thirst and toiling of the day;
But fired with hope and flushed with victory
Right manfully the Northmen did they ply.
Saxon and Dane and Angle knew full well
That with their fall their hearths and homesteads
    fell ;
Northman and Scot, that if the foeman won
Their last faint hope of life and home was gone.
So long and loud the storm of conflict raged,
And fast and furious was the battle waged ;

    But see ! it droops—the Berserk spirit and
        strength
That fired the North are failing them at length

    'Tis over now ; and now the fiercest foe
That England ever fought against is low.

THE SCULPTOR.

(WRITTEN WHEN A CHILD.)

I.

Where the yellow Tiber flows
   'Twixt the seven hills of Rome,
'Neath the purple Vatican,
   Stood a lowly sculptor's home.

II.

He was friendless, he was poor,
   But none had the sculptor's art
Truly as had Mellito,
   For he sculptured from his heart.

III.

Came a noble rich and great,
   'Sculptor, by thine art to me
Canst thou give a second child
   Half as beautiful to see?'

IV.

Said the sculptor to the lord,
   ' Should the noble lady deign
But to come to me, I could
   Recreate her to a vein.'

V.

Spake the lord, with father's pride,
   ' All you ask for shall be done,
That 1 may not be bereft,
   Childless, when my daughter's gone.'

VI.

Came the maiden day by day
   To the yellow river's side ;
Lifelike was the sculptor's work,
   For 'twas Love his tools did guide.

VII.

Till at last the work was done :
   Said the painter fervently,
' Let her sire the statue have,
   I must have her, or I die.'

VIII.

When she came to see his work,
   Fell the sculptor on his knee,
' Maiden fair, thou must be mine,
   Or else I must die for thee.'

IX.

Said the maiden scornfully,
  'Man, thy place thou dost not know ;
I but asked thee for my bust,
  Wherefore then address me so?'

X.

Said the sculptor, proud as she—
  'Thou thy bust shalt never have ;
Since I have not thee, thy form
  Shall be with me in the grave.'

XI.

Then he carved his name thereon,
  Dropped his chisel, seized a spade,
Dug a grave and threw it in,
  Killed himself where it was laid.

XII.

There the sculptor and his work
  Lay for ages out of sight,
Till some workmen digging deep,
  Brought the twain once more to light.

XIII.

Then, when ages had elapsed,
  Was the humble sculptor's name
Through the maid that shared his grave
  Blazoned on the scroll of fame.

ODE TO SOMNUS.

Father of gentle slumbers, and sweet dreams !
 Son of black night, and brother of pale Death !
Thou most sworn foe of Phœbus' orient beams,
 Whenc'er thy balmy fetters chain our breath
  The stormiest passions in our breasts are stilled,—
   The burdens of a lifetime are removed,
    And fancy free in pleasure's paths we
     roam ;
    And then, too, are fulfilled
   Our fondest hopes ; forbidden fruit we've
    loved
    Is ours, this once, until the daylight come.

In dreams the woods we love are ever green ;
 In dreams the forms we love are ever young ;
In dreams we ever haunt each best loved scene ;
 In dreams the selfsame chimes are ever rung
  That we remember ringing in our youth ;
   And Time, the truant, never, never flies ;
    And all we gaze upon seems ' home, sweet
     home.'

And all we hear seems truth,
As 't did in childhood : our enamoured eyes
Feast on their love until the daylight
come.

In dreams the lover clasps in ecstasy
  The loveliness that never may be his ;
And on the lips, that for another sigh,
  Imprints that earliest seal of love—a kiss.
    And cruel eyes most mercifully shine ;
      And cruel voices kindest words do sing ;
        And fairer forms than sculptor ever
          wrought,
        And beauty most divine,
      Fall to the lot of e'en the meanest thing
      That Nature mis-created in her sport.

In dreams the soldier rests, his warfare done,
  And clasps his absent wife in too-fond arms,
And tells his wondering boys of victories won,
  Nor recks of daily risks, and night alarms ;
    Nor hopes to hear the rolling of the drums ;
      Nor hopes to hear the morning bugle call,
      But thinks to rest in quiet all his days.
      The drum-beat never comes,
    The bugle never sounds, till all, till all
      Come truly with the sun's returning rays.

In dreams, what captive hates captivity?
  The gyves upon his wrists are children's hands,
And serve but to remind him he is free !
  The gyves upon his feet are Love's own bands
    That stay his ever-leaving home anew !
      The mourner's sorrow overjoyeth joy,
        And the dear dead haunt their accustomed
          spheres ;
          And none doth bid adieu ;
        And all is golden bliss without alloy ;
          And in one night crowd all the joys of years.

Dreams are the Poet's fatherland : in dreams
  The golden days of Saturn come again ;
Fair Nymphs inhabit all the woodland streams ;
  On all the earth sweet Peace and Plenty reign ;
    Vice and Misfortune are no longer rife ;
      The War-fiend hides his sting in flowery earth ;
        And good cheer ousts foul want, and joy
          ousts sorrow !
        Oh ! that such were my life !
      One summer day of pleasure, peace and mirth,
        Without ev'n one misgiving for the morrow.

THE VOYAGE OF LIFE.

Life is a voyage : at first we float
As in a mimic paper boat
   Upon a garden-ocean ;
The lightest drop of rain that falls,
The faintest breath of wind that calls
   The aspen leaf to motion,
Will overset that tiny craft,
The least ill wreck the young life-raft.

The life grows stronger : now we glide
In a stout skiff upon the tide
   Of some broad ocean-haven ;
Real waves come rolling in ashore,
We see the surge, we hear the roar
   Of wild sea-horses driven
By tempest-choristers from far
Against the opposing harbour bar.

Beyond the bar there lies the sea,
Deep and dark and broad and free,
   Now lovely in its quiet ;
A liquid amethyst outspread

To match the summer overhead,
  Now splendid in its riot,
Tossing its crest in savage glee,
But grander in its savag'ry.

Thou art a man now—out to sea,
And sail thy voyage manfully :
  Seest those beacons peering?
They mark the quicksand and the reef,
Shoal, sunken rock, and beetling cliff;
  But if thou heed thy steering,
And lose not heart, thou yet mayst reach,
With all hands saved, the one safe beach.

Life is as various as the trips
Of mariners in earthly ships
  To earthly harbours faring.
Some merchantmen that slowly sail,
But homeward bound, defy the gale
  Of India's ocean, bearing
Wares from the cradle of the day,
Or from mysterious Cathay.

Some river argosies, that pass
O'er inland waters smooth as glass,
  Laden with easy treasure ;
Or rich men's yachts that risk no harm

But only tempt the sea in calm,
　Their crew and cargo pleasure ;
A landsman's voyage, a woman's life
That never risks or storm or strife.

I would be a vessel of war
Sailing over the sea afar,
　Seeking not gain but glory ;
Manfully riding out the storm,
Dreading neither the iron form
　Of northern promontory,
Nor the terrible blasts that sweep
Over the face of the southern deep.

I would fight for God and the right
With fleets of the foe, nor dread their might ;
　And if they proved the stronger,
Never would I surrender or fly,
But fight until I might sink or die,
　No need then to live longer.
God grant I conquer, and reach at last
The port that knows not battle or blast.

LAMENT OF MDLLE. ——.

WHOSE FATHER AND LOVER WERE ARRESTED ON THE
SAME DAY BY ROBESPIERRE.

The lark that greets the day,
Carolling in heaven,
His tuneful head doth lay
By his mate's at even,
Nor doth she ever know what 'tis to be bereaven.

Wife of the toilsome hind,
That works betimes o' morning,
When dost thou fail to find
Joy by thy mate's returning
To share the few poor pence he mars his life in
earning.

I, only I, am lone
In my castle bower,
Me no lover's tone
Cheers at twilight's hour,
My mate is far away in heartless foeman's power.

On my father's lands
  By a cottage fire
Children clap their hands
  Round a rustic sire,
Nor list for other joy, or any pleasaunce higher.

In my father's park
  All the timid deer
Seek the stag at dark
  Nor any danger fear
If only he, their sire and antler'd lord, be near.

I, only I, am lone
  In my castle bower,
Me no father's tone
  Cheers at twilight's hour,
My sire is far away in heartless foeman's power.

THE WOMAN'S DRAMA.

(TO MY ELDEST SISTER ON HER WEDDING DAY.)

Sister, farewell ; the parting comes at last,
To-day the first act of your play is past :
God grant you have two only in your life,
The act of daughter, and the act of wife.

DEBEMUR MORTI, ETC.

(HORACE.)

Soft whispers die away, e'en as they're said ;
Sweet odours fly away ; fresh flowers fade;
Gold tresses turn to grey ; eyes lose their light ;
All that is fair to-day dies off to-night.

DROWNED.

In a homeward-bound ' liner '
    Passing the Nore,
A seaman from China
    Lustily swore
That now he was safe he would venture no more.

A rough Channel billow,
    Hearing his vow,
Said, ' I'll be thy pillow,
    Seaman, I trow,
Ere ever thy ship grate the quay with her bow.'

The quay she was grating ;
    His wife, young and sweet,
Was anxiously waiting
    The sound of his feet,
And his children were crowding their father to greet.

Their father was sleeping
    In a sea dell,
The Nereids were keeping
    His ocean couch well,
And the wave was his pillow that sounded his knell.

SPIRIT-TROTH.

A RONDEAU.

Frank and fair, with sunny hair
And beauty spiritual and rare,
   With eyes that never answer'd yet
   To any asking eyes they met,
And firm and faultless mouth, that ne'er
   Deign'd its unplighted troth forget,
   We shall meet though we have not met.
Where are you waiting me, O where,
        Frank and fair?
   But, darling, soon as e'er we meet
   Your eyes will well know how to greet;
Your lips untried will featly pair,
We shall be friends—of years, I swear,
   Ere the first happy hour shall fleet—
        Frank and fair!

POSTSCRIPTA.

A PRAYER.

I thank thee, Lord, that thou hast given
   So much to me of this world's good,
So little of the bitter leaven
   With which the loaf of life's imbued.
Yet wealth is nought, nor pow'r availeth,
   And happiness is not for me,
If but in this respect it faileth
   To have my darling safe with me.

There's no one loves a clear blue heaven
   Or summer-noontides more than I ;
I gladly change the starry seven
   For the Cross of the Southern sky.
No one more fain in spring's young hours
   Wanders in forest or in field ;
But what grace can the trees and flowers
   To me without my darling yield?

I always have loved dogs and horses,
    To guide with firm but facile rein
The uncomplaining friend that courses
    Beneath one's saddle o'er the plain ;
To pat the faithful friendly collie
    That eyes me every time I move ;
But these would fail to soothe me—wholly—
    Could I not have her whom I love.

And dear to me are Art and Beauty,
    In their Protean forms pourtray'd ;
And oft a true disciple's duty
    To Ruin's plaintive charms I've paid.
I love rich hues in blended tangles,
    And subtle streams delight my heart ;
But hues are harsh and music jangles
    When she and I have chanc'd to part.

There's an elixir found in glory
    That compensates for years of strife ;
To have my name go down in story
    Has been the lodestar of my life.
But fame is as the flow'rs that perish,
    And glory's golden crown is dim,
If she I swore to love and cherish
    Is not vouchsafed to me by Him.

A Prayer.

I pray thee, merciful Creator,
　To let my darling stay with me,
I pray thee by our Mediator,
　Who died himself to set us free.
And thou, who rais'dst up Jairus' daughter,
　Let her but sleep and rise up heal'd,
Touch with thy saving hand the water,
　Guard her with goodness as a shield.

EPILOGUE.

Australia sends this book of song
To England, not so much in hope
That it will take its place among

The brotherhood of wider scope,
But rather that it will be read
By those who take this volume up

Remembering where it was bred.
We cannot, in our youth, compare
With the full-grown and perfected

Poesy rear'd in English air,
'Mid sights and sounds that would inspire
Mere rhymsters with a noble care

And something of poetic fire.
We have no Tower in legend veil'd,
No green and gallant Devonshire,

Whence little bands of heroes sail'd
To win new worlds : no minster high
With effigies in armour mail'd,

And with the cross'd legs that imply
An old crusader buried there,
Like Robert, Duke of Normandy :

We have no hoary Westminster,
Entombing all a nation's best—
Great sovereign, gallant soldier,

Poet, and minister, and priest ;
We have no battlemented keep,
Too often with a shatter'd crest,

Or overwhelm'd in rugged heap
Of turf, which tells a mystic tale
Of magic treasures hidden deep,

Or fallen roof fantastical :
We have no ancient battlefield,
Where the plough turns up rusty mail,

Or English bow, or Scottish shield,
Or matchlock of the Civil War,
Or lance that Clifford's knights did wield :

We've had no great old warrior,
Fit subject for high tragedy
Or theme for epic orator.

We have no Avon winding by
The low-roof'd town, with its broadways,
That cradled Shakspere's infancy,

And where he came to end his days,
And with his kinsmen share a tomb :
There's nothing brighter in his bays

Than that he thus should choose to come,
Yet in his manhood's seeming prime,
Back to his humble childhood's home.

You must not judge this book of rhyme
By standard of the full-grown muse
Of our good Queen Victoria's time ;

But first in dusty tomes peruse
The rude verse of King Edward's reign,
When English first came into use ;

Or read what the American
Could write two centuries ago.
Down in the corner of the main,

Where this small sheaf of rhyme did grow,
We have not yet lived fifty years :
But as the swift hours onward flow,

We too shall breed poetic peers
For Arnold and for Tennyson ;
And, without vanity or fears,

Not shrink from competition
With Bryant, Whittier, and the rest
Who've made their country's lyre known

S

To Anglo-Saxon, east and west.
But, if I had my choice of lot
By any living bard possess'd,

I think I'd choose the patriot
And patriarchal Longfellow's ;
Who, after labour polyglot,

Yet takes not his well-earn'd repose :
He writes not like an architect.
With compasses and measure close,

Geometrically correct ;
Nor raves of scarlet thread and mouth
Of frenzy, ruth, and steed foam-fleckt,

Delirium, and draught and drouth,
And the foul sores and sins of love
Or leprous passions of the South ;

Nor does he, like the High-Art drove,
Severely strain the bounds of sense ;
Nor does he with loose bridle rove

Through a chance opening in the fence,
Into the uplands drear and dry
(To minds of less sublime pretence)

Of ethical philosophy.
And yet, where'er the English speech
Establishes its sovereignty,

There do his homely verses reach,
And lie about in ev'ry home
As well on far-east Fiji's beach,

Or where Hong-kong looks o'er the foam,
And in the lordly halls of Kent,
Or 'neath St. Paul's majestic dome
As on his native continent.

With eyes on him, I made these rhymes,
Could I succeed so far, content
To catch the echo of his chimes

Melbourne, January 1, 1882.

LONDON : PRINTED BY
SPOTTISWOODE AND CO., NEW-STREET SQUARE.
AND PARLIAMENT STREET

A LIST OF

KEGAN PAUL, TRENCH, & CO.'S

PUBLICATIONS.

12.81.

A LIST OF
KEGAN PAUL, TRENCH, & CO.'S
PUBLICATIONS.

ADAMS (F. O.), F.R.G.S.
The History of Japan. From the Earliest Period to the Present Time. New Edition, revised. 2 volumes. With Maps and Plans. Demy 8vo. Cloth, price 21s. each.

ADAMS (W. D.).
Lyrics of Love, from Shakespeare to Tennyson. Selected and arranged by. Fcap. 8vo. Cloth extra, gilt edges, price 3s. 6d.

ADAMSON (H. T.), B.D.
The Truth as it is in Jesus. Crown 8vo. Cloth, price 8s. 6d.

The Three Sevens. Crown 8vo. Cloth, price 5s. 6d.

ADAM ST. VICTOR.
The Liturgical Poetry of Adam St. Victor. From the text of GAUTIER. With Translations into English in the Original Metres, and Short Explanatory Notes. By DIGBY S. WRANGHAM, M.A. 3 vols. Crown 8vo. Printed on hand-made paper. Cloth, price 21s.

A. K. H. B.
From a Quiet Place. A New Volume of Sermons. Crown 8vo. Cloth, price 5s.

ALBERT (Mary).
Holland and her Heroes to the year 1585. An Adaptation from Motley's " Rise of the Dutch Republic." Small crown 8vo. Cloth, price, 4s. 6d.

ALLEN (Rev. R.), M.A.
Abraham ; his Life, Times, and Travels, 3,800 years ago. Second Edition. With Map. Post 8vo. Cloth, price 6s.

ALLEN (Grant), B.A.
Physiological Æsthetics. Large post 8vo. 9s.

ALLIES (T. W.), M.A.
Per Crucem ad Lucem. The Result of a Life. 2 vols. Demy 8vo. Cloth, price 25s.

A Life's Decision. Crown 8vo. Cloth, price 7s. 6d.

ANDERSON (Col. R. P.).
Victories and Defeats. An Attempt to explain the Causes which have led to them. An Officer's Manual. Demy 8vo. Cloth, price 14s.

ANDERSON (R. C.), C.E.
Tables for Facilitating the Calculation of every Detail in connection with Earthen and Masonry Dams. Royal 8vo. Cloth, price £2 2s.

ARCHER (Thomas).
About my Father's Business. Work amidst the Sick, the Sad, and the Sorrowing. Crown 8vo. Cloth, price 2s. 6d.

ARMSTRONG (Richard A.),B.A.
Latter-Day Teachers. Six Lectures. Small crown 8vo. Cloth, price 2s. 6d.

Army of the North German Confederation.
A Brief Description of its Organization, of the Different Branches of the Service and their *rôle* in War, of its Mode of Fighting, &c. &c. Translated from the Corrected Edition, by permission of the Author, by Colonel Edward Newdigate. Demy 8vo. Cloth, price 5s.

ARNOLD (Arthur).
Social Politics. Demy 8vo. Cloth, price 14s.

Free Land. Second Edition. Crown 8vo. Cloth, price 6s.

AUBERTIN (J. J.).

Camoens' Lusiads. Portuguese Text, with Translation by. With Map and Portraits. 2 vols. Demy 8vo. Price 30s.

Seventy Sonnets of Camoens'. Portuguese text and translation, with some original poems. Dedicated to Captain Richard F. Burton. Printed on hand-made paper. Cloth, bevelled boards, gilt top, price 7s. 6d.

Aunt Mary's Bran Pie. By the author of "St. Olave's." Illustrated. Cloth, price 3s. 6d.

AVIA.

The Odyssey of Homer Done into English Verse. Fcap. 4to. Cloth, price 15s.

BADGER (George Perry), D.C.L.

An English-Arabic Lexicon. In which the equivalents for English words and idiomatic sentences are rendered into literary and colloquial Arabic. Royal 4to. Cloth, price £9 9s.

BAGEHOT (Walter).

Some Articles on the Depreciation of Silver, and Topics connected with it. Demy 8vo. Price 5s.

The English Constitution. A New Edition, Revised and Corrected, with an Introductory Dissertation on Recent Changes and Events. Crown 8vo. Cloth, price 7s. 6d.

Lombard Street. A Description of the Money Market. Seventh Edition. Crown 8vo. Cloth, price 7s. 6d.

BAGOT (Alan).

Accidents in Mines : their Causes and Prevention. Crown 8vo. Cloth, price 6s.

BAKER (Sir Sherston, Bart.).

Halleck's International Law ; or Rules Regulating the Intercourse of States in Peace and War. A New Edition, Revised, with Notes and Cases. 2 vols. Demy 8vo. Cloth, price 38s.

BAKER (Sir Sherston, Bart.)— *continued.*

The Laws relating to Quarantine. Crown 8vo. Cloth, price 12s. 6d.

BALDWIN (Capt. J. H.), F.Z.S.

The Large and Small Game of Bengal and the North-Western Provinces of India. 4to. With numerous Illustrations. Second Edition. Cloth, price 21s.

BALLIN (Ada S. and F. L.).

A Hebrew Grammar. With Exercises selected from the Bible. Crown 8vo. Cloth, price 7s. 6d.

BANKS (Mrs. G. L.).

God's Providence House. New Edition. Crown 8vo. Cloth, price 3s. 6d.

Ripples and Breakers Poems. Square 8vo. Cloth, price 5s.

BARCLAY (Edgar).

Mountain Life in Algeria. Crown 4to. With numerous Illustrations by Photogravure. Cloth, price 16s.

BARLEE (Ellen).

Locked Out : a Tale of the Strike. With a Frontispiece. Royal 16mo. Cloth, price 1s. 6d.

BARNES (William).

An Outline of English Speechcraft. Crown 8vo. Cloth, price 4s.

Poems of Rural Life, in the Dorset Dialect. New Edition, complete in 1 vol. Crown 8vo. Cloth, price 8s. 6d.

Outlines of Redecraft (Logic). With English Wording. Crown 8vo. Cloth, price 3s.

BARTLEY (George C. T.).

Domestic Economy : Thrift in Every Day Life. Taught in Dialogues suitable for Children of all ages. Small crown 8vo. Cloth, limp, 2s.

BAUR (Ferdinand), Dr. Ph.

A Philological Introduction to Greek and Latin for Students. Translated and adapted from the German of. By C. KEGAN PAUL, M.A. Oxon., and the Rev. E. D. STONE, M.A., late Fellow of King's College, Cambridge, and Assistant Master at Eton. Second and revised edition. Crown 8vo. Cloth, price 6s.

BAYNES (Rev. Canon R. H.).

At the Communion Time. A Manual for Holy Communion. With a preface by the Right Rev. the Lord Bishop of Derry and Raphoe. Cloth, price 1s. 6d.
   ⁎⁎ Can also be had bound in French morocco, price 2s. 6d.; Persian morocco, price 3s.; Calf, or Turkey morocco, price 3s. 6d.

Home Songs for Quiet Hours. Fourth and Cheaper Edition. Fcap. 8vo Cloth, price 2s. 6d.
   This may also be had handsomely bound in morocco with gilt edges.

BELLINGHAM (Henry), Barrister-at-Law.

Social Aspects of Catholicism and Protestantism in their Civil Bearing upon Nations. Translated and adapted from the French of M. le Baron de Haulleville. With a Preface by His Eminence Cardinal Manning. Second and cheaper edition. Crown 8vo. Cloth, price 3s. 6d.

BENNETT (Dr. W. C.).

Narrative Poems & Ballads. Fcap. 8vo. Sewed in Coloured Wrapper, price 1s.

Songs for Sailors. Dedicated by Special Request to H. R. H. the Duke of Edinburgh. With Steel Portrait and Illustrations. Crown 8vo. Cloth, price 3s. 6d.
   An Edition in Illustrated Paper Covers, price 1s.

Songs of a Song Writer. Crown 8vo. Cloth, price 6s.

BENT (J. Theodore).

Genoa. How the Republic Rose and Fell. With 18 Illustrations. Demy 8vo. Cloth, price 18s.

BETHAM - EDWARDS (Miss M.).

Kitty. With a Frontispiece. Crown 8vo. Cloth, price 6s.

EEVINGTON (L. S.).

Key Notes. Small crown 8vo. Cloth, price 5s.

Blue Roses ; or, Helen Malinofska's Marriage. By the Author of "Véra." 2 vols. Fifth Edition. Cloth, gilt tops, 12s.
   ⁎⁎ Also a Cheaper Edition in 1 vol. With Frontispiece. Crown 8vo. Cloth, price 6s.

BLUME (Major W.).

The Operations of the German Armies in France, from Sedan to the end of the war of 1870-71. With Map. From the Journals of the Head-quarters Staff. Translated by the late E. M. Jones, Maj. 20th Foot, Prof. of Mil. Hist., Sandhurst. Demy 8vo. Cloth, price 9s.

BOGUSLAWSKI (Capt. A. von).

Tactical Deductions from the War of 1870-71. Translated by Colonel Sir Lumley Graham, Bart., late 18th (Royal Irish) Regiment. Third Edition, Revised and Corrected. Demy 8vo. Cloth, price 7s.

BONWICK (J.), F.R.G.S.

Egyptian Belief and Modern Thought. Large post 8vo. Cloth, price 10s. 6d.

Pyramid Facts and Fancies. Crown 8vo. Cloth, price 5s.

The Tasmanian Lily. With Frontispiece. Crown 8vo. Cloth, price 5s.

Mike Howe, the Bushranger of Van Diemen's Land. With Frontispiece. New and cheaper edition. Crown 8vo. Cloth, price 3s. 6d.

BOWEN (H. C.), M. A.

English Grammar for Beginners. Fcap. 8vo. Cloth, price 1s.

Studies in English, for the use of Modern Schools. Small crown 8vo. Cloth, price 1s. 6d.

Simple English Poems. English Literature for Junior Classes. In Four Parts. Parts I. and II., price 6d. each, now ready.

BOWRING (Sir John).
Autobiographical Recollections. With Memoir by Lewin B. Bowring. Demy 8vo. Price 14s.

Brave Men's Footsteps.
By the Editor of "Men who have Risen." A Book of Example and Anecdote for Young People. With Four Illustrations by C. Doyle. Sixth Edition. Crown 8vo. Cloth, price 3s. 6d.

BRIALMONT (Col. A.).
Hasty Intrenchments.
Translated by Lieut. Charles A. Empson, R.A. With Nine Plates. Demy 8vo. Cloth, price 6s.

BRIDGETT (Rev. J. E.).
History of the Holy Eucharist in Great Britain. 2 vols., demy 8vo. Cloth, price 18s.

BRODRICK (The Hon. G. C.).
Political Studies. Demy 8vo. Cloth, price 14s.

BROOKE (Rev. S. A.), M. A.
The Late Rev. F. W. Robertson, M.A., Life and Letters of. Edited by.
I. Uniform with the Sermons. 2 vols. With Steel Portrait. Price 7s. 6d.
II. Library Edition. 8vo. With Portrait. Price 12s.
III. A Popular Edition, in 1 vol. 8vo. Price 6s.
Sermons. First Series. Twelfth and Cheaper Edition. Crown 8vo. Cloth, price 5s.
Sermons. Second Series. Fifth and Cheaper Edition. Crown 8vo. Cloth, price 5s.
Theology in the English Poets. — COWPER, COLERIDGE, WORDSWORTH, and BURNS. Fourth and Cheaper Edition. Post 8vo. Cloth, price 5s.
Christ in Modern Life. Fifteenth and Cheaper Edition. Crown 8vo. Cloth. price 5s.
The Spirit of the Christian Life. A New Volume of Sermons. Second Edition. Crown 8vo. Cloth, price 7s. 6d.
The Fight of Faith. Sermons preached on various occasions. Fifth Edition. Crown 8vo. Cloth, price 7s. 6d.

BROOKE (W. G.), M. A.
The Public Worship Regulation Act. With a Classified Statement of its Provisions, Notes, and Index. Third Edition, Revised and Corrected. Crown 8vo. Cloth, price 3s. 6d.
Six Privy Council Judgments—1850-1872. Annotated by. Third Edition. Crown 8vo. Cloth, price 9s.

BROUN (J. A.).
Magnetic Observations at Trevandrum and Augustia Malley. Vol. I. 4to. Cloth, price 63s.
The Report from above, separately sewed, price 21s.

BROWN (Rev. J. Baldwin).
The Higher Life. Its Reality, Experience, and Destiny. Fifth and Cheaper Edition. Crown 8vo. Cloth, price 5s.
Doctrine of Annihilation in the Light of the Gospel of Love. Five Discourses. Third Edition. Crown 8vo. Cloth, price 2s. 6d.
The Christian Policy of Life. A Book for Young Men of Business. New and Cheaper Edition. Crown 8vo. Cloth, price 3s. 6d.

BROWN (J. Croumbie), LL.D.
Reboisement in France; or, Records of the Replanting of the Alps, the Cevennes, and the Pyrenees with Trees, Herbage, and Bush. Demy 8vo. Cloth, price 12s. 6d.
The Hydrology of Southern Africa. Demy 8vo. Cloth, price 10s. 6d.

BROWNE (W. R.).
The Inspiration of the New Testament. With a Preface by the Rev. J. P. NORRIS, D.D. Fcap. 8vo. Cloth, price 2s. 6d.

BRYANT (W. C.)
Poems. Red-line Edition. With 24 Illustrations and Portrait of the Author. Crown 8vo. Cloth extra, price 7s. 6d.
A Cheaper Edition, with Frontispiece. Small crown 8vo. Cloth, price 3s. 6d.

BURCKHARDT (Jacob).

The Civilization of the Period of the Renaissance in Italy. Authorized translation, by S. G. C. Middlemore. 2 vols. Demy 8vo. Cloth, price 24s.

BURTON (Mrs. Richard).

The Inner Life of Syria, Palestine, and the Holy Land. With Maps, Photographs, and Coloured Plates. 2 vols. Second Edition. Demy8vo. Cloth, price 24s.

** Also a Cheaper Edition in one volume. Large post 8vo. Cloth, price 10s. 6d.

BURTON (Capt. Richard F.).

The Gold Mines of Midian and the Ruined Midianite Cities. A Fortnight's Tour in North Western Arabia. With numerous Illustrations. Second Edition. Demy 8vo. Cloth, price 18s.

The Land of Midian Revisited. With numerous illustrations on wood and by Chromolithography. 2 vols. Demy 8vo. Cloth, price 32s.

BUSBECQ (Ogier Ghiselin de).

His Life and Letters. By Charles Thornton Forster, M.D. and F. H. Blackburne Daniell, M.D. 2 vols. With Frontispieces. Demy 8vo. Cloth, price 24s.

BUTLER (Alfred J.).

Amaranth and Asphodel. Songs from the Greek Anthology.— I. Songs of the Love of Women. II. Songs of the Love of Nature. III. Songs of Death. IV. Songs of Hereafter. Small crown 8vo. Cloth, price 2s.

CALDERON.

Calderon's Dramas: The Wonder-Working Magician—Life is a Dream—The Purgatory of St. Patrick. Translated by Denis Florence MacCarthy. Post 8vo. Cloth, price 10s.

CANDLER (H.).

The Groundwork of Belief. Crown 8vo. Cloth, price 7s.

CARPENTER (W. B.), M.D.

The Principles of Mental Physiology. With their Applications to the Training and Discipline of the Mind, and the Study of its Morbid Conditions. Illustrated. Fifth Edition. 8vo. Cloth, price 12s.

CARPENTER (Dr. Philip P.).

His Life and Work. Edited by his brother, Russell Lant Carpenter. With portrait and vignette. Second Edition. Crown 8vo. Cloth, price 7s. 6d.

CAVALRY OFFICER.

Notes on Cavalry Tactics, Organization, &c. With Diagrams Demy 8vo. Cloth, price 12s.

CERVANTES.

The Ingenious Knight Don Quixote de la Mancha. A New Translation from the Originals of 1605 and 1608. By A. J. Duffield. With Notes. 3 vols. demy 8vo. Cloth, price 42s.

CHAPMAN (Hon. Mrs. E. W.).

A Constant Heart. A Story. 2 vols. Cloth, gilt tops, price 12s.

CHEYNE (Rev. T. K.).

The Prophecies of Isaiah. Translated, with Critical Notes and Dissertations by. Two vols., demy 8vo. Cloth, price 25s.

Children's Toys, and some Elementary Lessons in General Knowledge which they teach. Illustrated. Crown 8vo. Cloth, price 5s.

Clairaut's Elements of Geometry. Translated by Dr. Kaines, with 145 figures. Crown 8vo. Cloth, price 4s. 6d.

CLARKE (Mary Cowden).

Honey from the Weed. Crown 8vo. Cloth, price 7s.

CLAYDEN (P. W.).

England under Lord Beaconsfield. The Political History of the Last Six Years, from the end of 1873 to the beginning of 1880. Second Edition. With Index, and Continuation to March, 1880. Demy 8vo. Cloth, price 16s.

CLERY (C.), Lieut.-Col.
Minor Tactics. With 26 Maps and Plans. Fifth and Revised Edition. Demy 8vo. Cloth, price 16s.

CLODD (Edward), F.R.A.S.
The Childhood of the World : a Simple Account of Man in Early Times. Sixth Edition. Crown 8vo. Cloth, price 3s.
A Special Edition for Schools. Price 1s.

The Childhood of Religions. Including a Simple Account of the Birth and Growth of Myths and Legends. Third Thousand. Crown 8vo. Cloth, price 5s.
A Special Edition for Schools. Price 1s. 6d.

Jesus of Nazareth. With a brief Sketch of Jewish History to the Time of His Birth. Small crown 8vo. Cloth, price 6s.

COGHLAN (J. Cole), D.D.
The Modern Pharisee and other Sermons. Edited by the Very Rev. A. H. Dickinson, D.D., Dean of Chapel Royal, Dublin. New and cheaper edition. Crown 8vo. Cloth, price 7s. 6d.

COLERIDGE (Sara).
Pretty Lessons in Verse for Good Children, with some Lessons in Latin, in Easy Rhyme. A New Edition. Illustrated. Fcap. 8vo. Cloth, price 3s. 6d.

Phantasmion. A Fairy Tale. With an Introductory Preface by the Right Hon. Lord Coleridge, of Ottery St. Mary. A New Edition. Illustrated. Crown 8vo. Cloth, price 7s. 6d.

Memoir and Letters of Sara Coleridge. Edited by her Daughter. Cheap Edition. With one Portrait. Cloth, price 7s. 6d.

COLLINS (Mortimer).
The Secret of Long Life. Small crown 8vo. Cloth, price 3s. 6d.
Inn of Strange Meetings, and other Poems. Crown 8vo. Cloth, price 5s.

CONNELL (A. K.).
Discontent and Danger in India. Small crown 8vo. Cloth, price 3s. 6d.

COOKE (Prof. J. P.)
Scientific Culture. Crown 8vo. Cloth, price 1s.

COOPER (H. J.).
The Art of Furnishing on Rational and Æsthetic Principles. New and Cheaper Edition. Fcap. 8vo. Cloth, price 1s. 6d.

COPPÉE (François).
L'Exilée. Done into English Verse with the sanction of the Author by I. O. L. Crown 8vo. Vellum, price 5s.

CORFIELD (Prof.), M.D.
Health. Crown 8vo. Cloth, price 6s.

CORY (Col. Arthur).
The Eastern Menace. Crown 8vo. Cloth, price 7s. 6d.

CORY (William).
A Guide to Modern English History. Part I. MDCCCXV.—MDCCCXXX. Demy 8vo. Cloth, price 9s.

COURTNEY (W. L.).
The Metaphysics of John Stuart Mill. Crown 8vo. Cloth, price 5s. 6d.

COX (Rev. Sir G. W.), Bart.
A History of Greece from the Earliest Period to the end of the Persian War. New Edition. 2 vols. Demy 8vo. Cloth, price 36s.

A General History of Greece from the Earliest Period to the Death of Alexander the Great, with a sketch of the subsequent History to the present time. New Edition. Crown 8vo. Cloth, price 7s. 6d.

Tales of Ancient Greece. New Edition. Small crown 8vo Cloth, price 6s.

School History of Greece. With Maps. New Edition. Fcap. 8vo. Cloth, price 3s. 6d.

The Great Persian War from the Histories of Herodotus. New Edition. Fcap. 8vo. Cloth, price 3s. 6d.

A Manual of Mythology in the form of Question and Answer New Edition. Fcap. 8vo. Cloth, price 3s.

COX (Rev. Sir G. W.), Bart.— *continued.*

An Introduction to the Science of Comparative Mythology and Folk-Lore. Large crown 8vo. Cloth, price 9s.

COX (Rev. Sir G. W.), Bart., M.A., and EUSTACE HINTON JONES.

Popular Romances of the Middle Ages. Second Edition in one volume. Crown 8vo. Cloth, price 6s.

COX (Rev. Samuel).

A Commentary on the Book of Job. With a Translation. Demy 8vo. Cloth, price 15s.

Salvator Mundi ; or, Is Christ the Saviour of all Men? Sixth Edition. Crown 8vo. Cloth, price 5s.

The Genesis of Evil, and other Sermons, mainly Expository. Second Edition. Crown 8vo. Cloth, price 6s.

CRAUFURD (A. H.).

Seeking for Light : Sermons. Crown 8vo. Cloth, price 5s.

CRAVEN (Mrs.).

A Year's Meditations. Crown 8vo. Cloth, price 6s.

CRAWFURD (Oswald).

Portugal, Old and New. With Illustrations and Maps. New and Cheaper Edition. Crown 8vo. Cloth, price 6s.

CRESSWELL (Mrs. G.).

The King's Banner. Drama in Four Acts. Five Illustrations. 4to. Cloth, price 10s. 6d.

CROZIER (John Beattie), M.B.

The Religion of the Future. Crown 8vo. Cloth, price 6s.

Cyclopædia of Common Things. Edited by the Rev. Sir GEORGE W. COX, Bart., M.A. With 500 Illustrations. Large post 8vo. Cloth, price 7s. 6d.

DALTON (John Neale), M.A., R.N.

Sermons to Naval Cadets. Preached on board H.M.S. "Britannia." Second Edition. Small crown 8vo. Cloth, price 3s. 6d.

D'ANVERS (N. R.).

Parted. A Tale of Clouds and Sunshine. With 4 Illustrations. Extra Fcap. 8vo. Cloth, price 3s. 6d.

Little Minnie's Troubles. An Every-day Chronicle. With Four Illustrations by W. H. Hughes. Fcap. Cloth, price 3s. 6d.

Pixie's Adventures ; or, the Tale of a Terrier. With 21 Illustrations. 16mo. Cloth, price 4s. 6d.

Nanny's Adventures ; or, the Tale of a Goat. With 12 Illustrations. 16mo. Cloth, price 4s. 6d.

DAVIDSON (Rev. Samuel), D.D., LL.D.

The New Testament, translated from the Latest Greek Text of Tischendorf. A New and thoroughly Revised Edition. Post 8vo. Cloth, price 10s. 6d.

Canon of the Bible : Its Formation, History, and Fluctuations. Third Edition, revised and enlarged. Small crown 8vo. Cloth, price 5s.

DAVIES (G. Christopher).

Rambles and Adventures of Our School Field Club. With Four Illustrations. New and Cheaper Edition. Crown 8vo. Cloth, price 3s. 6d.

DAVIES (Rev. J. L.), M.A.

Theology and Morality. Essays on Questions of Belief and Practice. Crown 8vo. Cloth, price 7s. 6d.

DAVIES (T. Hart.).

Catullus. Translated into English Verse. Crown 8vo. Cloth, price 6s.

DAWSON (George), M.A.

The Authentic Gospel. A New Volume of Sermons. Edited by GEORGE ST. CLAIR. Crown 8vo. Cloth, price 6s.

Prayers, with a Discourse on Prayer. Edited by his Wife. Sixth Edition. Crown 8vo. Price 6s.

DAWSON (George), M.A.—*continued.*

Sermons on Disputed Points and Special Occasions. Edited by his Wife. Third Edition. Crown 8vo. Cloth, price 6s.

Sermons on Daily Life and Duty. Edited by his Wife. Third Edition. Crown 8vo. Cloth, price 6s.

DE L'HOSTE (Col. E. P.).

The Desert Pastor, Jean Jarousseau. Translated from the French of Eugène Pelletan. With a Frontispiece. New Edition. Fcap. 8vo. Cloth, price 3s. 6d.

DE REDCLIFFE (Viscount Stratford), P.C., K.G., G.C.B.

Why am I a Christian? Fifth Edition. Crown 8vo. Cloth, price 3s.

DESPREZ (Philip S.).

Daniel and John; or, the Apocalypse of the Old and that of the New Testament. Demy 8vo. Cloth, price 12s.

DE TOCQUEVILLE (A.).

Correspondence and Conversations of, with Nassau William Senior, from 1834 to 1859. Edited by M. C. M. Simpson. 2 vols. Post 8vo. Cloth, price 21s.

DE VERE (Aubrey).

Legends of the Saxon Saints. Small crown 8vo. Cloth, price 6s.

Alexander the Great. A Dramatic Poem. Small crown 8vo. Cloth, price 5s.

The Infant Bridal, and other Poems. A New and Enlarged Edition. Fcap. 8vo. Cloth, price 7s. 6d.

The Legends of St. Patrick, and other Poems. Small crown 8vo. Cloth, price 5s.

St. Thomas of Canterbury. A Dramatic Poem. Large fcap. 8vo. Cloth, price 5s.

Antar and Zara: an Eastern Romance. INISFAIL, and other Poems, Meditative and Lyrical. Fcap. 8vo. Price 6s.

DE VERE (Aubrey)—*continued.*

The Fall of Rora, the Search after Proserpine, and other Poems, Meditative and Lyrical. Fcap. 8vo. Price 6s.

DOBELL (Mrs. Horace).

Ethelstone, Eveline, and other Poems. Crown 8vo. Cloth, price 6s.

DOBSON (Austin).

Vignettes in Rhyme and Vers de Société. Third Edition. Fcap. 8vo. Cloth, price 5s.

Proverbs in Porcelain. By the Author of "Vignettes in Rhyme." Second Edition. Crown 8vo. 6s.

Dorothy. A Country Story in Elegiac Verse. With Preface. Demy 8vo. Cloth, price 5s.

DOWDEN (Edward), LL.D.

Shakspere: a Critical Study of his Mind and Art. Fifth Edition. Large post 8vo. Cloth, price 12s.

Studies in Literature, 1789-1877. Large post 8vo. Cloth, price 12s.

Poems. Second Edition. Fcap. 8vo. Cloth, price 5s.

DOWNTON (Rev. H.), M.A.

Hymns and Verses. Original and Translated. Small crown 8vo. Cloth, price 3s. 6d.

DREWRY (G. O.), M.D.

The Common-Sense Management of the Stomach. Fifth Edition. Fcap. 8vo. Cloth, price 2s. 6d.

DREWRY (G. O.), M.D., and BARTLETT (H. C.), Ph.D., F.C.S.

Cup and Platter: or, Notes on Food and its Effects. New and cheaper Edition. Small 8vo. Cloth, price 1s. 6d.

DRUMMOND (Miss).

Tripps Buildings. A Study from Life, with Frontispiece. Small crown 8vo. Cloth, price 3s. 6d.

DUFFIELD (A. J.).
Don Quixote. His Critics and Commentators. With a Brief Account of the Minor Works of Miguel de Cervantes Saavedra, and a statement of the end and aim of the greatest of them all. A Handy Book for General Readers. Crown 8vo. Cloth, price 3s. 6d.

DU MONCEL (Count).
The Telephone, the Microphone, and the Phonograph. With 74 Illustrations. Small crown 8vo. Cloth, price 5s.

DUTT (Toru).
A Sheaf Gleaned in French Fields. New Edition, with Portrait. Demy 8vo. Cloth, price 10s. 6d.

DU VERNOIS (Col. von Verdy).
Studies in leading Troops. An authorized and accurate Translation by Lieutenant H. J. T. Hildyard, 71st Foot. Parts I. and II. Demy 8vo. Cloth, price 7s.

EDEN (Frederick).
The Nile without a Dragoman. Second Edition. Crown 8vo. Cloth, price 7s. 6d.

EDGEWORTH (F. Y.).
Mathematical Psychics: an Essay on the Application of Mathematics to Social Science. Demy 8vo. Cloth, price 7s. 6d.

EDIS (Robert W.).
Decoration and Furniture of Town Houses. A series of Cantor Lectures delivered before the Society of Arts, 1880. Amplified and enlarged, with 29 full-page Illustrations and numerous sketches. Second Edition. Square 8vo. Cloth, price 12s. 6d.

EDMONDS (Herbert).
Well Spent Lives : a Series of Modern Biographies. New and Cheaper Edition. Crown 8vo. Price 3s. 6d.

Educational Code of the Prussian Nation, in its Present Form. In accordance with the Decisions of the Common Provincial Law, and with those of Recent Legislation. Crown 8vo. Cloth, price 2s. 6d.

THE EDUCATION LIBRARY (Edited by Philip Magnus).
An Introduction to the History of Educational Theories. By Oscar Browning, M.A. Cloth, price 3s. 6d.
John Amos Comenius : his Life and Educational Work. By Prof. S. S. Laurie, A.M. Cloth, price 3s. 6d.
Old Greek Education. By the Rev. Prof. Mahaffy, M.A. Cloth, price 3s. 6d.

EDWARDS (Rev. Basil).
Minor Chords; or, Songs for the Suffering: a Volume of Verse. Fcap. 8vo. Cloth, price 3s. 6d. ; paper, price 2s. 6d.

ELLIOT (Lady Charlotte).
Medusa and other Poems. Crown 8vo. Cloth, price 6s.

ELLIOTT (Ebenezer), The Corn Law Rhymer.
Poems. Edited by his Son, the Rev. Edwin Elliott, of St. John's, Antigua. 2 vols. Crown 8vo. Cloth, price 18s.

ELSDALE (Henry).
Studies in Tennyson's Idylls. Crown 8vo. Cloth, price 5s.

ELYOT (Sir Thomas).
The Boke named the Gouernour. Edited from the First Edition of 1531 by Henry Herbert Stephen Croft, M.A., Barrister-at-Law. With Portraits of Sir Thomas and Lady Elyot, copied by permission of her Majesty from Holbein's Original Drawings at Windsor Castle. 2 vols. fcap. 4to. Cloth, price 50s.

Epic of Hades (The).
By the author of "Songs of Two Worlds." Twelfth Edition. Fcap. 8vo. Cloth, price 7s. 6d.
*** Also an Illustrated Edition with seventeen full-page designs in photomezzotint by George R. Chapman. 4to. Cloth, extra gilt leaves, price 25s. and a Large Paper Edition, with portrait, price 10s. 6d.

EVANS (Anne).
Poems and Music. With Memorial Preface by Ann Thackeray Ritchie. Large crown 8vo. Cloth, price 7s. 6d.

EVANS (Mark).

The Gospel of Home Life. Crown 8vo. Cloth, price 4s. 6d.

The Story of our Father's Love, told to Children. Fourth and Cheaper Edition. With Four Illustrations. Fcap. 8vo. Cloth, price 1s. 6d.

A Book of Common Prayer and Worship for Household Use, compiled exclusively from the Holy Scriptures. New and Cheaper Edition. Fcap. 8vo. Cloth, price 1s.

The King's Story Book. In three parts. Fcap. 8vo. Cloth, price 1s. 6d. each.
₊ Parts I. and II., with eight illustrations and two Picture Maps, now ready.

EX-CIVILIAN.

Life in the Mofussil; or, Civilian Life in Lower Bengal. 2 vols. Large post 8vo. Price 14s.

FARQUHARSON (M.).

I. Elsie Dinsmore. Crown 8vo. Cloth, price 3s. 6d.

II. Elsie's Girlhood. Crown 8vo. Cloth, price 3s. 6d.

III. Elsie's Holidays at Roselands. Crown 8vo. Cloth, price 3s. 6d.

FELKIN (H. M.).
Technical Education in a Saxon Town. Published for the City and Guilds of London Institute for the Advancement of Technical Education. Demy 8vo. Cloth, price 2s.

FIELD (Horace), B.A. Lond.
The Ultimate Triumph of Christianity. Small crown 8vo. Cloth, price 3s. 6d.

FINN (the late James), M.R.A.S.
Stirring Times; or, Records from Jerusalem Consular Chronicles of 1853 to 1856. Edited and Compiled by his Widow. With a Preface by the Viscountess STRANGFORD. 2 vols. Demy 8vo. Price 30s.

FLOREDICE (W. H.).
A Month among the Mere Irish. Small crown 8vo. Cloth, price 5s.

Folkestone Ritual Case (The). The Argument, Proceedings Judgment, and Report, revised by the several Counsel engaged. Demy 8vo. Cloth, price 25s.

FORMBY (Rev. Henry).
Ancient Rome and its Connection with the Christian Religion: an Outline of the History of the City from its First Foundation down to the Erection of the Chair of St. Peter, A.D. 42-47. With numerous Illustrations of Ancient Monuments, Sculpture, and Coinage, and of the Antiquities of the Christian Catacombs. Royal 4to. Cloth extra, price 50s. Roxburgh, half-morocco, price 52s. 6d.

FOWLE (Rev. T. W.), M.A.
The Reconciliation of Religion and Science. Being Essays on Immortality, Inspiration, Miracles, and the Being of Christ. Demy 8vo. Cloth, price 10s. 6d.

The Divine Legation of Christ. Crown 8vo. Cloth, price 7s.

FRASER (Donald).
Exchange Tables of Sterling and Indian Rupee Currency, upon a new and extended system, embracing Values from One Farthing to One Hundred Thousand Pounds, and at Rates progressing, in Sixteenths of a Penny, from 1s. 9d. to 2s. 3d. per Rupee. Royal 8vo. Cloth, price 10s. 6d.

FRISWELL (J. Hain).
The Better Self. Essays for Home Life. Crown 8vo. Cloth, price 6s.

One of Two; or, A Left-Handed Bride. With a Frontispiece. Crown 8vo. Cloth, price 3s. 6d.

GARDINER (Samuel R.) and J. BASS MULLINGER, M.A.
Introduction to the Study of English History. Large crown 8vo. Cloth, price 9s.

GARDNER (J.), M.D.
Longevity: The Means of Prolonging Life after Middle Age. Fourth Edition, Revised and Enlarged. Small crown 8vo. Cloth, price 4s.

GARRETT (E.).
By Still Waters. A Story for Quiet Hours. With Seven Illustrations. Crown 8vo. Cloth, price 6s.

GEBLER (Karl Von).
Galileo Galilei and the Roman Curia, from Authentic Sources. Translated with the sanction of the Author, by Mrs. GEORGE STURGE. Demy 8vo. Cloth, price 12s.

GEDDES (James).
History of the Administration of John de Witt, Grand Pensionary of Holland. Vol. I. 1623—1654. Demy 8vo., with Portrait. Cloth, price 15s.

GENNA (E.).
Irresponsible Philanthropists. Being some Chapters on the Employment of Gentlewomen. Small crown 8vo. Cloth, price 2s. 6d.

GEORGE (Henry).
Progress and Poverty. An Inquiry into the Cause of Industrial Depressions and of Increase of Want with Increase of Wealth. The Remedy. Post 8vo. Cloth, price 7s. 6d.

GILBERT (Mrs.).
Autobiography and other Memorials. Edited by Josiah Gilbert. Third Edition. With Portrait and several Wood Engravings. Crown 8vo. Cloth, price 7s. 6d.

GLOVER (F.), M.A.
Exempla Latina. A First Construing Book with Short Notes, Lexicon, and an Introduction to the Analysis of Sentences. Fcap. 8vo. Cloth, price 2s.

GODWIN (William).
William Godwin: His Friends and Contemporaries. With Portraits and Facsimiles of the handwriting of Godwin and his Wife. By C. Kegan Paul. 2 vols. Demy 8vo. Cloth, price 28s.

The Genius of Christianity Unveiled. Being Essays never before published. Edited, with a Preface, by C. Kegan Paul. Crown 8vo. Cloth, price 7s. 6d.

GOETZE (Capt. A. von).
Operations of the German Engineers during the War of 1870-1871. Published by Authority, and in accordance with Official Documents. Translated from the German by Colonel G. Graham, V.C., C.B., R.E. With 6 large Maps. Demy 8vo. Cloth, price 21s.

GOLDSMID (Sir Francis Henry).
Memoir of. With Portrait. Crown 8vo. Cloth, price 5s.

GOODENOUGH (Commodore J. G.), R.N., C.B., C.M.G.
Memoir of, with Extracts from his Letters and Journals. Edited by his Widow. With Steel Engraved Portrait. Square 8vo. Cloth, 5s.
*** Also a Library Edition with Maps, Woodcuts, and Steel Engraved Portrait. Square post 8vo. Cloth, price 14s.

GOSSE (Edmund W.).
Studies in the Literature of Northern Europe. With a Frontispiece designed and etched by Alma Tadema. Large post 8vo. Cloth, price 12s.

New Poems. Crown 8vo. Cloth, price 7s. 6d.

GOULD (Rev. S. Baring), M.A.
Germany, Present and Past. New and Cheaper Edition. Large crown 8vo. Cloth, price 7s. 6d.

The Vicar of Morwenstow: a Memoir of the Rev. R. S. Hawker. With Portrait. Third Edition, revised. Square post 8vo. Cloth, price 10s. 6d.

GRAHAM (William), M.A.
The Creed of Science : Religious, Moral, and Social. Demy 8vo. Cloth, price 12s.

GRIFFITH (Thomas), A.M.
The Gospel of the Divine Life. A Study of the Fourth Evangelist. Demy 8vo. Cloth, price 14s.

GRIMLEY (Rev. H. N.), M.A.
Tremadoc Sermons, chiefly on the SPIRITUAL BODY, the UNSEEN WORLD, and the DIVINE HUMANITY. Second Edition. Crown 8vo. Cloth, price 6s.

GRÜNER (M. L.).
Studies of Blast Furnace Phenomena. Translated by L. D. B. Gordon, F.R.S.E., F.G.S. Demy 8vo. Cloth, price 7s. 6d.

GURNEY (Rev. Archer).
Words of Faith and Cheer. A Mission of Instruction and Suggestion. Crown 8vo. Cloth, price 6s.

Gwen : A Drama in Monologue. By the Author of the "Epic of Hades." Third Edition. Fcap. 8vo. Cloth, price 5s.

HAECKEL (Prof. Ernst).
The History of Creation. Translation revised by Professor E. Ray Lankester, M.A., F.R.S. With Coloured Plates and Genealogical Trees of the various groups of both plants and animals. 2 vols. Second Edition. Post 8vo. Cloth, price 32s.

The History of the Evolution of Man. With numerous Illustrations. 2 vols. Large post 8vo. Cloth, price 32s.

Freedom in Science and Teaching. From the German of Ernst Haeckel, with a Prefatory Note by T. H. Huxley, F.R.S. Crown 8vo. Cloth, price 5s.

HALF-CROWN SERIES.
Sister Dora : a Biography. By Margaret Lonsdale.
True Words for Brave Men. A Book for Soldiers and Sailors. By the late Charles Kingsley.
An Inland Voyage. By R. L. Stevenson.
Travels with a Donkey. By R. L. Stevenson.
A Nook in the Apennines. By Leader Scott.
Notes of Travel. Being Extracts from the Journals of Count Von Moltke.
Letters from Russia. By Count Von Moltke.
English Sonnets. Collected and Arranged by J. Dennis.
Lyrics of Love from Shakespeare to Tennyson. Selected and Arranged by W. D. Adams.
London Lyrics. By Frederick Locker.

HALF-CROWN SERIES — *continued.*
Home Songs for Quiet Hours. By the Rev. Canon R. H. Baynes.

Halleck's International Law ; or, Rules Regulating the Intercourse of States in Peace and War. A New Edition, revised, with Notes and Cases. By Sir Sherston Baker, Bart. 2 vols. Demy 8vo. Cloth, price 38s.

HARDY (Thomas).
A Pair of Blue Eyes. New Edition. With Frontispiece. Crown 8vo. Cloth, price 6s.
The Return of the Native. New Edition. With Frontispiece. Crown 8vo. Cloth, price 6s.

HARRISON (Lieut.-Col. R.).
The Officer's Memorandum Book for Peace and War. Third Edition. Oblong 32mo. roan, with pencil, price 3s. 6d.

HARTINGTON (The Right Hon. the Marquis of), M.P.
Election Speeches in 1879 and 1880. With Address to the Electors of North-East Lancashire. Crown 8vo. Cloth, price 3s. 6d.

HAWEIS (Rev. H. R.), M.A.
Arrows in the Air. Crown 8vo. Fourth and Cheaper Edition. Cloth, price 5s.
Current Coin. Materialism— The Devil—Crime—Drunkenness— Pauperism—Emotion—Recreation— The Sabbath. Fourth and Cheaper Edition. Crown 8vo. Cloth, price 5s.
Speech in Season. Fifth and Cheaper Edition. Crown 8vo. Cloth, price 5s.
Thoughts for the Times. Twelfth and Cheaper Edition. Crown 8vo. Cloth, price 5s.
Unsectarian Family Prayers. New and Cheaper Edition. Fcap. 8vo. Cloth, price 1s. 6d.

HAWKER (Robert Stephen).
The Poetical Works of. Now first collected and arranged with a prefatory notice by J. G. Godwin. With Portrait. Crown 8vo. Cloth, price 12s.

HAWKINS (Edwards Comerford).
Spirit and Form. Sermons preached in the parish church of Leatherhead. Crown 8vo. Cloth, price 6s.

HAYES (A. H.).
New Colorado and the Santa Fé Trail. With map and 60 Illustrations. Crown 8vo. Cloth, price 9s.

HEIDENHAIN (Rudolf), M.D.
Animal Magnetism. Physiological Observations. Translated from the Fourth German Edition, by L. C. Wooldridge. With a Preface by G. R. Romanes, F.R.S. Crown 8vo. Cloth, price 2s. 6d.

HELLON (H. G.).
Daphnis. A Pastoral Poem. Small crown 8vo. Cloth.

HELLWALD (Baron F. von).
The Russians in Central Asia. A Critical Examination, down to the present time, of the Geography and History of Central Asia. Translated by Lieut.-Col. Theodore Wirgman, LL.B. Large post 8vo. With Map. Cloth, price 12s.

HELVIG (Major H.).
The Operations of the Ba- varian Army Corps. Translated by Captain G. S. Schwabe. With Five large Maps. In 2 vols. Demy 8vo. Cloth, price 24s.

Tactical Examples: Vol. I. The Battalion, price 15s. Vol. II. The Regiment and Brigade, price 10s. 6d. Translated from the German by Col. Sir Lumley Graham. With numerous Diagrams. Demy 8vo. Cloth.

HERFORD (Brooke).
The Story of Religion in England. A Book for Young Folk. Crown 8vo. Cloth, price 5s.

HICKEY (E. H.).
A Sculptor and other Poems. Small crown 8vo. Cloth, price 5s.

HINTON (James).
Life and Letters of. Edited by Ellice Hopkins, with an Introduction by Sir W. W. Gull, Bart., and Portrait engraved on Steel by C. H. Jeens. Fourth Edition. Crown 8vo. Cloth, 8s. 6d.

Chapters on the Art of Thinking, and other Essays. With an Introduction by Shadworth Hodgson. Edited by C. H. Hinton. Crown 8vo. Cloth, price 8s. 6d.

The Place of the Physician. To which is added ESSAYS ON THE LAW OF HUMAN LIFE, AND ON THE RELATION BETWEEN ORGANIC AND INORGANIC WORLDS. Second Edition. Crown 8vo. Cloth, price 3s. 6d.

Physiology for Practical Use. By various Writers. With 50 Illustrations. Third and cheaper edition. Crown 8vo. Cloth, price 5s.

An Atlas of Diseases of the Membrana Tympani. With Descriptive Text. Post 8vo. Price £6 6s.

The Questions of Aural Surgery. With Illustrations. 2 vols. Post 8vo. Cloth, price 12s. 6d.

The Mystery of Pain. New Edition. Fcap. 8vo. Cloth limp, 1s.

HOCKLEY (W. B.).
Tales of the Zenana; or, A Nuwab's Leisure Hours. By the Author of "Pandurang Hari." With a Preface by Lord Stanley of Alderley. 2 vols. Crown 8vo. Cloth, price 21s.

Pandurang Hari; or, Memoirs of a Hindoo. A Tale of Mahratta Life sixty years ago. With a Preface by Sir H. Bartle E. Frere, G.C.S.I., &c. New and Cheaper Edition. Crown 8vo. Cloth, price 6s.

HOFFBAUER (Capt.).
The German Artillery in the Battles near Metz. Based on the official reports of the German Artillery. Translated by Capt. E. O. Hollist. With Map and Plans. Demy 8vo. Cloth, price 21s.

HOLMES (E. G. A.).
Poems. First and Second Series. Fcap. 8vo. Cloth, price 5s. each.

HOOPER (Mary).

Little Dinners: How to Serve them with Elegance and Economy. Thirteenth Edition. Crown 8vo. Cloth, price 5s.

Cookery for Invalids, Per- sons of Delicate Digestion, and Children. Crown 8vo. Cloth, price 3s. 6d.

Every-Day Meals. Being Economical and Wholesome Recipes for Breakfast, Luncheon, and Supper. Second Edition. Crown 8vo. Cloth, price 5s.

HOOPER (Mrs. G.).

The House of Raby. With a Frontispiece. Crown 8vo. Cloth, price 3s. 6d.

HORNER (The Misses).

Walks in Florence. A New and thoroughly Revised Edition. 2 vols. Crown 8vo. Cloth limp. With Illustrations.
Vol. I.—Churches, Streets, and Palaces. 10s. 6d. Vol. II.—Public Galleries and Museums. 5s.

Household Readings on Prophecy. By a Layman. Small crown 8vo. Cloth, price 3s. 6d.

HUGHES (Henry).

The Redemption of the World. Crown 8vo. Cloth, price 3s 6d.

HULL (Edmund C. P.).

The European in India. With a MEDICAL GUIDE FOR ANGLO-INDIANS. By R. R. S. Mair, M.D., F.R.C.S.E. Third Edition, Revised and Corrected. Post 8vo. Cloth, price 6s.

HUTCHISON (Lieut.-Col. F. J.), and Capt. G. H. MACGREGOR.

Military Sketching and Re- connaissance. With Fifteen Plates. Second edition. Small 8vo. Cloth, price 6s.
The first Volume of Military Handbooks for Regimental Officers. Edited by Lieut.-Col. C. B. BRACKENBURY, R.A., A.A.G.

HUTTON (Arthur), M.A.

The Anglican Ministry. Its Nature and Value in relation to the Catholic Priesthood. With a Preface by his Eminence Cardinal Newman. Demy 8vo. Cloth, price 14s.

INCHBOLD (J. W.).

Annus Amoris. Sonnets. Fcap. 8vo. Cloth, price 4s. 6d.

INGELOW (Jean).

Off the Skelligs. A Novel. With Frontispiece. Second Edition. Crown 8vo. Cloth, price 6s.

The Little Wonder-horn. A Second Series of "Stories Told to a Child." With Fifteen Illustrations. Small 8vo. Cloth, price 2s. 6d.

International Scientific Series (The). Each book complete in one Volume. Crown 8vo. Cloth, price 5s. each, excepting those marked otherwise.

I. **Forms of Water:** A Familiar Exposition of the Origin and Phenomena of Glaciers. By J. Tyndall, LL.D., F.R.S. With 25 Illustrations. Eighth Edition.

II. **Physics and Politics;** or, Thoughts on the Application of the Principles of "Natural Selection" and "Inheritance" to Political Society. By Walter Bagehot. Fifth Edition. Crown 8vo. Cloth, price 4s.

III. **Foods.** By Edward Smith, M.D., &c. With numerous Illustrations. Seventh Edition.

IV. **Mind and Body:** The Theories of their Relation. By Alexander Bain, LL.D. With Four Illustrations. Tenth Edition. Crown 8vo. Cloth, price 4s.

V. **The Study of Sociology.** By Herbert Spencer. Tenth Edition.

VI. **On the Conservation of** Energy. By Balfour Stewart, LL.D., &c. With 14 Illustrations. Fifth Edition.

VII. **Animal Locomotion;** or, Walking, Swimming, and Flying. By J. B. Pettigrew, M.D., &c. With 130 Illustrations. Second Edition.

VIII. **Responsibility in Mental** Disease. By Henry Maudsley, M.D. Third Edition.

IX. **The New Chemistry.** By Professor J. P. Cooke. With 31 Illustrations. Fifth Edition.

X. **The Science of Law.** By Prof. Sheldon Amos. Fourth Edition.

International Scientific Series (The)—*continued.*

XI. **Animal Mechanism.** A Treatise on Terrestrial and Aerial Locomotion. By Prof. E. J. Marey. With 117 Illustrations. Second Edition.

XII. **The Doctrine of Descent and Darwinism.** By Prof. Osca Schmidt. With 26 Illustrations. Fourth Edition.

XIII. **The History of the Conflict between Religion and Science.** By J. W. Draper, M.D., LL.D. Fifteenth Edition.

XIV. **Fungi; their Nature, Influences, Uses,** &c. By M. C. Cooke, LL.D. Edited by the Rev. M. J. Berkeley, F.L.S. With numerous Illustrations. Second Edition.

XV. **The Chemical Effects of Light and Photography.** By Dr. Hermann Vogel. With 100 Illustrations. Third and Revised Edition.

XVI. **The Life and Growth of Language.** By Prof. William Dwight Whitney. Third Edition.

XVII. **Money and the Mechanism of Exchange.** By W. Stanley Jevons, F.R.S. Fourth Edition.

XVIII. **The Nature of Light:** With a General Account of Physical Optics. By Dr. Eugene Lommel. With 188 Illustrations and a table of Spectra in Chromo-lithography. Third Edition.

XIX. **Animal Parasites and Messmates.** By M. Van Beneden. With 83 Illustrations. Second Edition.

XX. **Fermentation.** By Prof. Schützenberger. With 28 Illustrations. Third Edition.

XXI. **The Five Senses of Man.** By Prof. Bernstein. With 91 Illustrations. Second Edition.

XXII. **The Theory of Sound in its Relation to Music.** By Prof. Pietro Blaserna. With numerous Illustrations. Second Edition.

XXIII. **Studies in Spectrum Analysis.** By J. Norman Lockyer. F.R.S. With six photographic Illustrations of Spectra, and numerous engravings on wood. Crown 8vo. Second Edition. 6s. 6d.

International Scientific Series (The)—*continued.*

XXIV. **A History of the Growth of the Steam Engine.** By Prof. R. H. Thurston. With numerous Illustrations. Second Edition. 6s. 6d.

XXV. **Education as a Science.** By Alexander Bain, LL.D. Third Edition.

XXVI. **The Human Species.** By Prof. A. de Quatrefages. Third Edition.

XXVII. **Modern Chromatics.** With Applications to Art and Industry, by Ogden N. Rood. With 130 original Illustrations. Second Edition.

XXVIII. **The Crayfish:** an Introduction to the Study of Zoology. By Prof. T. H. Huxley. With eighty-two Illustrations. Third edition.

XXIX. **The Brain as an Organ of Mind.** By H. Charlton Bastian, M.D. With numerous Illustrations. Second Edition.

XXX. **The Atomic Theory.** By Prof. Ad. Wurtz. Translated by E. Clemin-Shaw. Second Edition.

XXXI. **The Natural Conditions of Existence as they affect Animal Life.** By Karl Semper. Second Edition.

XXXII. **General Physiology of Muscles and Nerves.** By Prof. J. Rosenthal. With Illustrations. Second Edition.

XXXIII. **Sight:** an Exposition of the Principles of Monocular and Binocular Vision. By Joseph Le Conte, LL.D. With 132 illustrations.

XXXIV. **Illusions:** A Psychological Study. By James Sully.

XXXV. **Volcanoes:** What they are and What they Teach. By Prof. J. W. Judd, F.R.S. With 92 Illustrations on Wood.

XXXVI. **Suicide.** An Essay in Comparative Mythology. By Prof. E. Morselli, with Diagrams.

XXXVII. **The Brain and its Functions.** By J. Luys. With numerous illustrations.

JENKINS (E.) and RAYMOND (J.). The Architect's Legal Handbook. Third Edition Revised. Crown 8vo. Cloth, price 6s.

JENKINS (Rev. R. C.), M.A.
The Privilege of Peter and the Claims of the Roman Church confronted with the Scriptures, the Councils, and the Testimony of the Popes themselves. Fcap. 8vo. Cloth, price 3s. 6d.

JENNINGS (Mrs. Vaughan).
Rahel : Her Life and Letters. With a Portrait from the Painting by Daffinger. Square post 8vo. Cloth, price 7s. 6d.

JOEL (L.).
A Consul's Manual and Shipowner's and Shipmaster's Practical Guide in their Transactions Abroad. With Definitions of Nautical, Mercantile, and Legal Terms ; a Glossary of Mercantile Terms in English, French, German, Italian, and Spanish. Tables of the Money, Weights, and Measures of the Principal Commercial Nations and their Equivalents in British Standards ; and Forms of Consular and Notarial Acts. Demy 8vo. Cloth, price 12s.

JOHNSON (Virginia W.).
The Catskill Fairies. Illustrated by Alfred Fredericks. Cloth, price 5s.

JOHNSTONE (C. F.), M.A.
Historical Abstracts. Being Outlines of the History of some of the less-known States of Europe. Crown 8vo. Cloth, price 7s. 6d.

JONES (Lucy).
Puddings and Sweets. Being Three Hundred and Sixty-Five Receipts approved by Experience. Crown 8vo., price 2s. 6d.

JOYCE (P. W.), LL.D., &c.
Old Celtic Romances. Translated from the Gaelic by. Crown 8vo. Cloth, price 7s. 6d.

KAUFMANN (Rev. M.), B.A.
Utopias ; or, Schemes of Social Improvement, from Sir Thomas More to Karl Marx. Crown 8vo. Cloth, price 5s.

Socialism : Its Nature, its Dangers, and its Remedies considered. Crown 8vo. Cloth, price 7s.6d.

KAY (Joseph), M.A., Q.C.
Free Trade in Land. Edited by his Widow. With Preface by the Right Hon. John Bright, M.P. Sixth Edition. Crown 8vo. Cloth, price 5s.

KEMPIS (Thomas à).
Of the Imitation of Christ. Parchment Library Edition, price 6s.; vellum, price 7s 6d.
. A Cabinet Edition is also published at 1s. 6d. and a Miniature Edition at 1s. These may also be had in various extra bindings.

KENT (Carolo).
Corona Catholica ad Petri successoris Pedes Oblata. De Summi Pontificis Leonis XIII. Assumptione Epiggramma. In Quinquaginta Linguis. Fcap. 4to. Cloth, price 15s.

KER (David).
The Boy Slave in Bokhara. A Tale of Central Asia. With Illustrations. Crown 8vo. Cloth, price 3s. 6d.
The Wild Horseman of the Pampas. Illustrated. Crown 8vo. Cloth, price 3s. 6d.

KERNER (Dr. A.), Professor of Botany in the University of Innsbruck.
Flowers and their Unbidden Guests. Translation edited by W. OGLE, M.A., M.D., and a prefatory letter by C. Darwin, F.R.S. With Illustrations. Sq. 8vo. Cloth, price 9s.

KIDD (Joseph), M.D.
The Laws of Therapeutics, or, the Science and Art of Medicine. Second Edition. Crown 8vo. Cloth, price 6s.

KINAHAN (G. Henry), M.R.I.A., &c., of her Majesty's Geological Survey.
Manual of the Geology of Ireland. With 8 Plates, 26 Woodcuts, and a Map of Ireland, geologically coloured. Square 8vo. Cloth, price 15s.

KING (Mrs. Hamilton).
The Disciples. Fourth Edition, with Portrait and Notes. Crown 8vo. Cloth, price 7s. 6d.
Aspromonte, and other Poems. Second Edition. Fcap. 8vo. Cloth, price 4s. 6d.

KINGSFORD (Anna), M.D.
The Perfect Way in Diet.
A Treatise advocating a Return to the Natural and Ancient Food of Race. Small crown 8vo. Cloth, price 2s.

KINGSLEY (Charles), M.A.
Letters and Memories of his Life. Edited by his WIFE. With 2 Steel engraved Portraits and numerous Illustrations on Wood, and a Facsimile of his Handwriting. Thirteenth Edition. 2 vols. Demy 8vo. Cloth, price 36s.

⁎ Also the eleventh Cabinet Edition in 2 vols. Crown 8vo. Cloth, price 12s.

All Saints' Day and other Sermons. Second Edition. Crown 8vo. Cloth, 7s. 6d.

True Words for Brave Men: a Book for Soldiers' and Sailors' Libraries. Eighth Edition. Crown 8vo. Cloth, price 2s. 6d.

KNIGHT (Professor W.).
Studies in Philosophy and Literature. Large post 8vo. Cloth, price 7s. 6d.

KNOX (Alexander A.).
The New Playground : or, Wanderings in Algeria. Large crown 8vo. Cloth, price 10s. 6d.

LAMONT (Martha MacDonald).
The Gladiator: A Life under the Roman Empire in the beginning of the Third Century. With four Illustrations by H. M. Paget. Extra fcap. 8vo. Cloth, price 3s. 6d.

LANG (A.).
XXXII Ballades in Blue China. Elzevir. 8vo. Parchment, price 5s.

LAYMANN (Capt.).
The Frontal Attack of Infantry. Translated by Colonel Edward Newdigate. Crown 8vo. Cloth, price 2s. 6d.

LEANDER (Richard).
Fantastic Stories. Translated from the German by Paulina B. Granville. With Eight full-page Illustrations by M. E. Fraser-Tytler. Crown 8vo. Cloth, price 5s.

LEE (Rev. F. G.), D.C.L.
The Other World; or, Glimpses of the Supernatural. 2 vols. A New Edition. Crown 8vo. Cloth, price 15s.

LEE (Holme).
Her Title of Honour. A Book for Girls. New Edition. With a Frontispiece. Crown 8vo. Cloth, price 5s.

LEWIS (Edward Dillon).
A Draft Code of Criminal Law and Procedure. Demy 8vo. Cloth, price 21s.

LEWIS (Mary A.).
A Rat with Three Tales. New and cheaper edition. With Four Illustrations by Catherine F. Frere. Crown 8vo. Cloth, price 3s. 6d.

LINDSAY (W. Lauder), M.D., &c.
Mind in the Lower Animals in Health and Disease. 2 vols. Demy 8vo. Cloth, price 32s.

LOCKER (F.).
London Lyrics. A New and Revised Edition, with Additions and a Portrait of the Author. Crown 8vo. Cloth, elegant, price 6s. Also a Cheap Edition, price 2s. 6d.

LOKI.
The New Werther. Small crown 8vo. Cloth, price 2s. 6d.

LORIMER (Peter), D.D.
John Knox and the Church of England: His Work in her Pulpit, and his Influence upon her Liturgy, Articles, and Parties. Demy 8vo. Cloth, price 12s.

John Wiclif and his English Precursors, by Gerhard Victor Lechler. Translated from the German, with additional Notes. New and Cheaper Edition. Demy 8vo. Cloth, price 10s. 6d.

Love Sonnets of Proteus. With frontispiece by the Author. Elzevir 8vo. Cloth, price 5s.

Lowder (Charles) : a Biography. By the author of "St. Teresa." Large crown 8vo. With Portrait. Cloth, price 7s. 6d.

LOWNDES (Henry).
Poems and Translations.
Crown 8vo. Cloth, price 6s.

LUMSDEN (Lieut.-Col. H. W.).
Beowulf. An Old English
Poem. Translated into modern
rhymes. Small crown 8vo. Cloth,
price 5s.

MAC CLINTOCK (L.).
Sir Spangle and the Dingy
Hen. Illustrated. Square crown
8vo., price 2s. 6d.

MACDONALD (G.).
Malcolm. With Portrait of
the Author engraved on Steel. Fourth
Edition. Crown 8vo. Price 6s.

The Marquis of Lossie.
Second Edition. Crown 8vo. Cloth,
price 6s.

St. George and St. Michael.
Second Edition. Crown 8vo. Cloth, 6s.

MACKENNA (S. J.).
Plucky Fellows. A Book
for Boys. With Six Illustrations.
Fourth Edition. Crown 8vo. Cloth,
price 3s. 6d.

At School with an Old
Dragoon. With Six Illustrations.
Second Edition. Crown 8vo. Cloth,
price 5s.

MACLACHLAN (Mrs.).
Notes and Extracts on
Everlasting Punishment and
Eternal Life, according to
Literal Interpretation. Small
crown 8vo. Cloth, price 3s. 6d.

MACLEAN (Charles Donald).
Latin and Greek Verse
Translations. Small crown 8vo.
Cloth, price 2s.

MACNAUGHT (Rev. John).
Cœna Domini: An Essay
on the Lord's Supper, its Primi-
tive Institution, Apostolic Uses,
and Subsequent History. Demy
8vo. Cloth, price 14s.

MAGNUS (Mrs.).
About the Jews since Bible
Times. From the Babylonian exile
till the English Exodus. Small
crown 8vo. Cloth, price 6s.

MAGNUSSON (Eiríkr), M.A.,
and PALMER (E.H.), M.A.
Johan Ludvig Runeberg's
Lyrical Songs, Idylls and Epi-
grams. Fcap. 8vo. Cloth, price 5s.

MAIR (R. S.), M.D., F.R.C.S.E.
The Medical Guide for
Anglo-Indians. Being a Compen-
dium of Advice to Europeans in
India, relating to the Preservation
and Regulation of Health. With a
Supplement on the Management of
Children in India. Second Edition.
Crown 8vo. Limp cloth, price 3s. 6d.

MALDEN (H. E. and E. E.)
Princes and Princesses.
Illustrated. Small crown 8vo. Cloth,
price 2s. 6d.

MANNING (His Eminence Car-
dinal).
The True Story of the
Vatican Council. Crown 8vo.
Cloth, price 5s.

MARKHAM (Capt. Albert Hastings), R.N.
The Great Frozen Sea. A
Personal Narrative of the Voyage of
the "Alert" during the Arctic Expedition of 1875-6. With six full-
page Illustrations, two Maps, and
twenty-seven Woodcuts. Fourth
and cheaper edition. Crown 8vo.
Cloth, price 6s.

A Polar Reconnaissance:
being the Voyage of the "Isbjorn"
to Novaya Zemlya in 1879. With
10 Illustrations. Demy 8vo. Cloth,
price 16s.

Marriage and Maternity; or,
Scripture Wives and Mothers.
Small crown 8vo. Cloth, price 4s. 6d.

MARTINEAU (Gertrude).
Outline Lessons on
Morals. Small crown 8vo. Cloth,
price 3s. 6d.

Master Bobby: a Tale. By
the Author of "Christina North."
With Illustrations by E. H. BELL.
Extra fcap. 8vo. Cloth, price 3s. 6d.

MASTERMAN (J.).
Half-a-dozen Daughters.
With a Frontispiece. Crown 8vo.
Cloth, price 3s. 6d.

McGRATH (Terence).

Pictures from Ireland. New and cheaper edition. Crown 8vo. Cloth, price 2s.

MEREDITH (George).

The Egoist. A Comedy in Narrative. 3 vols. Crown 8vo. Cloth.

*** Also a Cheaper Edition, with Frontispiece. Crown 8vo. Cloth, price 6s.

The Ordeal of Richard Feverel. A History of Father and Son. In one vol. with Frontispiece. Crown 8vo. Cloth, price 6s.

MEREDITH (Owen) [the Earl of Lytton].

Lucile. With 160 Illustrations. Crown 4to. cloth extra, gilt leaves, price 21s.

MERRITT (Henry).

Art - Criticism and Romance. With Recollections, and Twenty-three Illustrations in *eau-forte*, by Anna Lea Merritt. Two vols. Large post 8vo. Cloth, 25s.

MIDDLETON (The Lady).

Ballads. Square 16mo. Cloth, price 3s. 6d.

MILLER (Edward).

The History and Doctrines of Irvingism; or, the so-called Catholic and Apostolic Church. 2 vols. Large post 8vo. Cloth, price 25s.

The Church in Relation to the State. Crown 8vo. Cloth, price 7s. 6d.

MILNE (James).

Tables of Exchange for the Conversion of Sterling Money into Indian and Ceylon Currency, at Rates from 1s. 8d. to 2s. 3d. per Rupee. Second Edition. Demy 8vo. Cloth, price £2 2s.

MOCKLER (E.).

A Grammar of the Baloo- chee Language, as it is spoken in Makran (Ancient Gedrosia), in the Persia-Arabic and Roman characters. Fcap. 8vo. Cloth, price 5s.

MOFFAT (Robert Scott).

The Economy of Consump- tion; an Omitted Chapter in Political Economy, with special reference to the Questions of Commercial Crises and the Policy of Trades Unions; and with Reviews of the Theories of Adam Smith, Ricardo, J. S. Mill, Fawcett, &c. Demy 8vo. Cloth, price 18s.

The Principles of a Time Policy: being an Exposition of a Method of Settling Disputes between Employers and Employed in regard to Time and Wages, by a simple Process of Mercantile Barter, without recourse to Strikes or Locks-out. Demy 8vo. Cloth, price 3s. 6d.

MORELL (J. R.).

Euclid Simplified in Me- thod and Language. Being a Manual of Geometry. Compiled from the most important French Works, approved by the University of Paris and the Minister of Public Instruction. Fcap. 8vo. Cloth, price 2s. 6d.

MORSE (E. S.), Ph.D.

First Book of Zoology. With numerous Illustrations. New and cheaper edition. Crown 8vo. Cloth, price 2s. 6d.

MORSHEAD (E. D. A.)

The House of Atreus. Being the Agamemnon Libation-Bearers and Furies of Æschylus Translated into English Verse. Crown 8vo. Cloth, price 7s.

MUNRO (Major-Gen. Sir Thomas), K.C.B., Governor of Madras.

Selections from His Minutes, and other Official Writings. Edited, with an Introductory Memoir, by Sir Alexander Arbuthnot, K.C.S.I., C.I.E. Two vols. Demy 8vo. Cloth, price 30s.

NAAKE (J. T.).

Slavonic Fairy Tales. From Russian, Servian, Polish, and Bohemian Sources. With Four Illustrations. Crown 8vo. Cloth, price 5s.

NELSON (J. H.).

A Prospectus of the Scien- tific Study of the Hindû Law. Demy 8vo. Cloth, price 9s.

NEWMAN (J. H.), D.D.
Characteristics from the Writings of. Being Selections from his various Works. Arranged with the Author's personal approval. Third Edition. With Portrait. Crown 8vo. Cloth, price 6s.
*** A Portrait of the Rev. Dr. J. H. Newman, mounted for framing, can be had, price 2s. 6d.

NICHOLAS (Thomas), Ph.D., F.G.S.
The Pedigree of the English People: an Argument, Historical and Scientific, on the Formation and Growth of the Nation, tracing Race-admixture in Britain from the earliest times, with especial reference to the incorporation of the Celtic Aborigines. Fifth Edition. Demy 8vo. Cloth, price 16s.

NICHOLSON (Edward Byron).
The Christ Child, and other Poems. Crown 8vo. Cloth, price 4s. 6d.

The Rights of an Animal. Crown 8vo. Cloth, price 3s. 6d.

The Gospel according to the Hebrews. Its Fragments translated and annotated, with a critical Analysis of the External and Internal Evidence relating to it. Demy 8vo. Cloth, price 9s. 6d.

A New Commentary on the Gospel according to Matthew. Demy 8vo. Cloth, price 12s.

NICOLS (Arthur), F.G.S., F.R.G.S.
Chapters from the Physical History of the Earth. An Introduction to Geology and Palæontology, with numerous illustrations. Crown 8vo. Cloth, price 5s.

NOAKE (Major R. Compton).
The Bivouac ; or, Martial Lyrist, with an Appendix—Advice to the Soldier. Fcap. 8vo. Price 5s. 6d.

NOEL (The Hon. Roden).
A Little Child's Monument. Third Edition. Small crown 8vo. Cloth, price 3s. 6d.

NORMAN PEOPLE (The).
The Norman People, and their Existing Descendants in the British Dominions and the United States of America. Demy 8vo. Cloth, price 21s.

NORRIS (Rev. Alfred).
The Inner and Outer Life Poems. Fcap. 8vo. Cloth, price 6s.

Notes on Cavalry Tactics, Organization, &c. By a Cavalry Officer. With Diagrams. Demy 8vo. Cloth, price 12s.

Nuces : Exercises on the Syntax of the Public School Latin Primer. New Edition in Three Parts. Crown 8vo. Each 1s.
*** The Three Parts can also be had bound together in cloth, price 3s.

OATES (Frank), F.R.G.S.
Matabele Land and the Victoria Falls: A Naturalist's Wanderings in the Interior of South Africa. Edited by C. G. Oates, B.A., with numerous illustrations and four maps. Demy 8vo. Cloth, price 21s.

O'BRIEN (Charlotte G.).
Light and Shade. 2 vols. Crown 8vo. Cloth, gilt tops, price 12s.

Ode of Life (The).
Third Edition. Fcap. 8vo. Cloth, price 5s.

OF THE IMITATION OF CHRIST. Four Books. Cabinet Edition, price 1s. and 1s. 6d., cloth; Miniature Edition, price 1s.
*** Also in various bindings.

O'HAGAN (John).
The Song of Roland. Translated into English Verse. Large post 8vo. Parchment antique, price 10s. 6d.

O'MEARA (Kathleen).
Frederic Ozanam, Professor of the Sorbonne: His Life and Works. Second Edition. Crown 8vo. Cloth, price 7s. 6d.

Henri Perreyve and His Counsels to the Sick. Small crown 8vo. Cloth, price 5s.

OTTLEY (Henry Bickersteth).
The Great Dilemma: Christ
His own Witness or His own
Accuser. Six Lectures. Crown 8vo.
Cloth, price 3s. 6d.

Our Public Schools. Eton,
Harrow, Winchester, Rugby, Westminster, Marlborough, The Charter-
house. Crown 8vo. Cloth, price 6s.

OWEN (F. M.).
John Keats. A Study.
Crown 8vo. Cloth, price 6s.

OWEN (Rev. Robert), B.D.
Sanctorale Catholicum : or
Book of Saints. With Notes, Criti-
cal, Exegetical, and Historical.
Demy 8vo. Cloth, price 18s.

An Essay on the Commu-
nion of Saints. Including an
Examination of the "Cultus Sanc-
torum." Price 2s.

PALGRAVE (W. Gifford).
Hermann Agha ; An Eastern
Narrative. Third and Cheaper Edi-
tion. Crown 8vo. Cloth, price 6s.

PANDURANG HARI ;
Or, Memoirs of a Hindoo.
With an Introductory Preface by Sir
H. Bartle E. Frere, G.C.S.I., C.B.
Crown 8vo. Price 6s.

PARCHMENT LIBRARY
(The).
Choicely printed on hand-made
paper, limp parchment antique, price
6s. each ; vellum, price 7s. 6d. each.
Edgar Allan Poe's Poems.
With an Essay on his Poetry by
ANDREW LANG and a frontispiece
by Linley Sambourne.

Shakspere's Sonnets.
Edited by Edward Dowden. With
a Frontispiece, etched by Leopold
Lowenstam, after the Death Mask.

English Odes. Selected by
Edmund W. Gosse. With Frontis-
piece on India paper by Hamo
Thornycroft, A.R.A.

OF THE IMITATION
OF CHRIST. Four Books. A
revised Translation. With Frontispiece on India paper, from a Design
by W. B. Richmond.

PARCHMENT LIBRARY (The)
—*continued.*
Tennyson's The Princess :
a Medley. With a Miniature Frontispiece by H. M. Paget, and a Tail-
piece in Outline by Gordon Browne.

Poems : Selected from Percy
Bysshe Shelley. Dedicated to Lady
Shelley. With Preface by Richard
Garnet, and a Miniature Frontis-
piece.

Tennyson's "In Memo-
riam." With a Miniature Portrait
in *eau forte* by Le Rat, after a
Photograph by the late Mrs. Cameron.

PARKER (Joseph), D.D.
The Paraclete : An Essay
on the Personality and Ministry of
the Holy Ghost, with some reference
to current discussions. Second Edition. Demy 8vo. Cloth, price 12s.

PARR (Capt. H. Hallam).
A Sketch of the Kafir and
Zulu Wars: Guadana to Isand-
hlwana, with Maps. Small crown
8vo. Cloth, price 5s.

The Dress, Horses, and
Equipment of Infantry and Staff
Officers. Crown 8vo. Cloth,
price 1s.

PARSLOE (Joseph).
Our Railways : Sketches,
Historical and Descriptive. With
Practical Information as to Fares,
Rates, &c., and a Chapter on Rail-
way Reform. Crown 8vo. Cloth,
price 6s.

PATTISON (Mrs. Mark).
The Renaissance of Art in
France. With Nineteen Steel
Engravings. 2 vols. Demy 8vo.
Cloth, price 32s.

PAUL (C. Kegan).
Mary Wollstonecraft.
Letters to Imlay. With Prefatory
Memoir by, and Two Portraits in
eau forte, by Anna Lea Merritt.
Crown 8vo. Cloth, price 6s.

Goethe's Faust. A New
Translation in Rime. Crown 8vo.
Cloth, price 6s.

PAUL (C. Kegan)—*continued.*
William Godwin: His Friends and Contemporaries. With Portraits and Facsimiles of the Handwriting of Godwin and his Wife. 2 vols. Square post 8vo. Cloth, price 28s.

The Genius of Christianity Unveiled. Being Essays by William Godwin never before published. Edited, with a Preface, by C. Kegan Paul. Crown 8vo. Cloth, price 7s. 6d.

PAUL (Margaret Agnes).
Gentle and Simple: A Story. 2 vols. Crown 8vo. Cloth, gilt tops, price 12s.
*** Also a Cheaper Edition in one vol. with Frontispiece. Crown 8vo. Cloth, price 6s.

PAYNE (John).
Songs of Life and Death. Crown 8vo. Cloth, price 5s.

PAYNE (Prof. J. F.).
Fröbel and the Kindergarten System. Second Edition.

A Visit to German Schools: Elementary Schools in Germany. Crown 8vo. Cloth, price 4s. 6d.

PELLETAN (E.).
The Desert Pastor, Jean Jarousseau. Translated from the French. By Colonel E. P. De L'Hoste. With a Frontispiece. New Edition. Fcap. 8vo. Cloth, price 3s. 6d.

PENNELL (H. Cholmondeley).
Pegasus Resaddled. By the Author of "Puck on Pegasus," &c. &c. With Ten Full-page Illustrations by George Du Maurier. Second Edition. Fcap. 4to. Cloth elegant, price 12s. 6d.

PENRICE (Maj. J.), B.A.
A Dictionary and Glossary of the Ko-ran. With copious Grammatical References and Explanations of the Text. 4to. Cloth, price 21s.

PESCHEL (Dr. Oscar).
The Races of Man and their Geographical Distribution. Large crown 8vo. Cloth, price 9s.

PETERS (F. H.).
The Nicomachean Ethics of Aristotle. Translated by. Crown 8vo. Cloth, price 6s.

PFEIFFER (Emily).
Under the Aspens. Lyrical and Dramatic. Crown 8vo. With Portrait. Cloth, price 6s.

Quarterman's Grace, and other Poems. Crown 8vo. Cloth, price 5s.

Glan Alarch: His Silence and Song. A Poem. Second Edition. Crown 8vo. price 6s.

Gerard's Monument, and other Poems. Second Edition. Crown 8vo. Cloth, price 6s.

Poems. Second Edition. Crown 8vo. Cloth, price 6s.

Sonnets and Songs. New Edition. 16mo, handsomely printed and bound in cloth, gilt edges, price 5s.

PIKE (Warburton).
The Inferno of Dante Alighieri. Demy 8vo. Cloth, price 5s.

PINCHES (Thomas), M.A.
Samuel Wilberforce: Faith —Service—Recompense. Three Sermons. With a Portrait of Bishop Wilberforce (after a Photograph by Charles Watkins). Crown 8vo. Cloth, price 4s. 6d.

PLAYFAIR (Lieut.-Col.), Her Britannic Majesty's Consul-General in Algiers.
Travels in the Footsteps of Bruce in Algeria and Tunis. Illustrated by facsimiles of Bruce's original Drawings, Photographs, Maps, &c. Royal 4to. Cloth, bevelled boards, gilt leaves, price £3 3s.

POLLOCK (Frederick).
Spinoza. His Life and Philosophy. Demy 8vo. Cloth, price 16s.

POLLOCK (W. H.).
Lectures on French Poets. Delivered at the Royal Institution. Small crown 8vo. Cloth, price 5s.

POOR (Laura E.).

Sanskrit and its kindred Literatures. Studies in Comparative Mythology. Small crown 8vo Cloth, price 5s.

POUSHKIN (A. S.).

Russian Romance. Translated from the Tales of Belkin, &c. By Mrs. J. Buchan Telfer (*née* Mouravieff). Crown 8vo. Cloth, price 3s. 6d.

PRESBYTER.

Unfoldings of Christian Hope. An Essay showing that the Doctrine contained in the Damnatory Clauses of the Creed commonly called Athanasian is unscriptural. Small crown 8vo. Cloth, price 4s. 6d.

PRICE (Prof. Bonamy).

Currency and Banking. Crown 8vo. Cloth, price 6s.

Chapters on Practical Political Economy. Being the Substance of Lectures delivered before the University of Oxford. Large post 8vo. Cloth, price 12s.

Proteus and Amadeus. A Correspondence. Edited by Aubrey De Vere. Crown 8vo. Cloth, price 5s.

PUBLIC SCHOOLBOY.

The Volunteer, the Militiaman, and the Regular Soldier. Crown 8vo. Cloth, price 5s.

PULPIT COMMENTARY (The).

Edited by the Rev. J. S. EXELL and the Rev. Canon H. D. M. SPENCE.

Genesis. By Rev. T. Whitelaw, M.A.; with Homilies by the Very Rev. J. F. Montgomery, D.D., Rev. Prof. R. A. Redford, M.A., LL.B., Rev. F. Hastings, Rev. W. Roberts, M.A. An Introduction to the Study of the Old Testament by the Rev. Canon Farrar, D.D., F.R.S.; and Introductions to the Pentateuch by the Right Rev. H. Cotterill, D.D., and Rev. T. Whitelaw, M.A. Fifth Edition. Price 15s.

PULPIT COMMENTARY (The) —*continued*.

Numbers. By the Rev. R. Winterbotham, LL.B. With Homilies by the Rev. Prof. W. Binnie, D.D., Rev. E. S. Prout, M.A., Rev. D. Young, Rev. J. Waite, and an Introduction by the Rev. Thomas Whitelaw, M.A. Third Edition. Price 15s.

Joshua. By the Rev. J. J. Lias, M.A. With Homilies by the Rev. S. R. Aldridge, LL.B., Rev. R. Glover, Rev. E. de Pressensé, D.D., Rev. J. Waite, Rev. F. W. Adeney, and an Introduction by the Rev. A. Plummer, M.A. Third Edition. Price 12s. 6d.

Judges and Ruth. By Right Rev. Lord A. C. Hervey, D.D., and Rev. J. Morrison, D.D. With Homilies by Rev. A. F. Muir, M.A.; Rev. W. F. Adeney, M.A.; Rev. W. M. Statham; and Rev. Prof. J. R. Thomson, M.A. Third Edition. Cloth, price 15s.

1 Samuel. By the Very Rev. R. P. Smith, D.D. With Homilies by the Rev. Donald Fraser, D.D., Rev. Prof. Chapman, and Rev. B. Dale. Fourth Edition. Price 15s.

1 Kings. By the Rev. Joseph Hammond, LL.B. With Homilies by the Rev. E. de Pressensé, D.D., Rev. J. Waite, B.A., Rev. A. Rowland, LL.B., Rev. J. A. Macdonald, and Rev. J. Urquhart.

Ezra, Nehemiah, and Esther. By Rev. Canon G. Rawlinson, M.A.; with Homilies by Rev. Prof. J. R. Thomson, M.A., Rev. Prof. R. A. Redford, LL.B., M.A., Rev. W. S. Lewis, M.A., Rev. J. A. Macdonald, Rev. A. Mackennal, B.A., Rev. W. Clarkson, B.A., Rev. F. Hastings, Rev. W. Dinwiddie, LL.B., Rev. Prof. Rowlands, B.A., Rev. G. Wood, B.A., Rev. Prof. P. C. Barker, LL.B., M.A., and Rev. J. S. Exell. Fifth Edition. Price 12s. 6d.

Punjaub (The) and North Western Frontier of India. By an old Punjaubee. Crown 8vo. Cloth, price 5s.

Rabbi Jeshua. An Eastern Story. Crown 8vo. Cloth, price 3s. 6d.

RADCLIFFE (Frank R. Y.).
The New Politicus. Small crown 8vo. Cloth, price 2s. 6d.

RAVENSHAW (John Henry), B.C.S.
Gaur: Its Ruins and Inscriptions. Edited with considerable additions and alterations by his Widow. With forty-four photographic illustrations and twenty-five fac-similes of Inscriptions. Super royal 4to. Cloth, 3l. 13s. 6d.

READ (Carveth).
On the Theory of Logic: An Essay. Crown 8vo. Cloth, price 6s.

Realities of the Future Life. Small crown 8vo. Cloth, price 1s. 6d.

REANEY (Mrs. G. S.).
Blessing and Blessed; a Sketch of Girl Life. New and cheaper Edition. With a frontispiece. Crown 8vo. Cloth, price 3s. 6d.

Waking and Working; or, from Girlhood to Womanhood. New and cheaper edition. With a Frontispiece. Crown 8vo. Cloth, price 3s. 6d.

Rose Gurney's Discovery. A Book for Girls, dedicated to their Mothers. Crown 8vo. Cloth, price 3s. 6d.

English Girls: their Place and Power. With a Preface by R. W. Dale, M.A., of Birmingham. Third Edition. Fcap. 8vo. Cloth, price 2s. 6d.

Just Anyone, and other Stories. Three Illustrations. Royal 16mo. Cloth, price 1s. 6d.

Sunshine Jenny and other Stories. Three Illustrations. Royal 16mo. Cloth, price 1s. 6d.

Sunbeam Willie, and other Stories. Three Illustrations. Royal 16mo. Cloth, price 1s. 6d.

RENDALL (J. M.).
Concise Handbook of the Island of Madeira. With plan of Funchal and map of the Island. Fcap. 8vo. Cloth, price 1s. 6d.

REYNOLDS (Rev. J. W.).
The Supernatural in Nature. A Verification by Free Use of Science. Second Edition, revised and enlarged. Demy 8vo. Cloth, price 14s.

Mystery of Miracles, The. By the Author of "The Supernatural in Nature." New and Enlarged Edition. Crown 8vo. Cloth, price 6s.

RHOADES (James).
The Georgics of Virgil. Translated into English Verse. Small crown 8vo. Cloth, price 5s.

RIBOT (Prof. Th.).
English Psychology. Second Edition. A Revised and Corrected Translation from the latest French Edition. Large post 8vo. Cloth, price 9s.

Heredity: A Psychological Study on its Phenomena, its Laws, its Causes, and its Consequences. Large crown 8vo. Cloth, price 9s.

RINK (Chevalier Dr. Henry).
Greenland: Its People and its Products. By the Chevalier Dr. HENRY RINK, President of the Greenland Board of Trade. With sixteen Illustrations, drawn by the Eskimo, and a Map. Edited by Dr. ROBERT BROWN. Crown 8vo. Price 10s. 6d.

ROBERTSON (The Late Rev. F. W.), M.A., of Brighton.
The Human Race, and other Sermons preached at Cheltenham, Oxford, and Brighton. Second Edition. Large post 8vo. Cloth, price 7s. 6d.

Notes on Genesis. New and cheaper Edition. Crown 8vo., price 3s. 6d.

Sermons. Four Series. Small crown 8vo. Cloth, price 3s. 6d. each.

Expository Lectures on St. Paul's Epistles to the Corinthians. A New Edition. Small crown 8vo. Cloth, price 5s.

Lectures and Addresses, with other literary remains. A New Edition. Crown 8vo. Cloth, price 5s.

ROBERTSON (The Late Rev. F. W.), M.A., of Brighton—*continued*.

An Analysis of Mr. Tennyson's "In Memoriam." (Dedicated by Permission to the Poet-Laureate.) Fcap. 8vo. Cloth, price 2s.

The Education of the Human Race. Translated from the German of Gotthold Ephraim Lessing. Fcap. 8vo. Cloth, price 2s. 6d.

Life and Letters. Edited by the Rev. Stopford Brooke, M.A., Chaplain in Ordinary to the Queen. I. 2 vols., uniform with the Sermons. With Steel Portrait. Crown 8vo. Cloth, price 7s. 6d. II. Library Edition, in Demy 8vo., with Portrait. Cloth, price 12s. III. A Popular Edition, in one vol. Crown 8vo. Cloth, price 6s.

The above Works can also be had half-bound in morocco.

** A Portrait of the late Rev. F. W. Robertson, mounted for framing, can be had, price 2s. 6d.

ROBINSON (A. Mary F.).

A Handful of Honeysuckle. Fcap. 8vo. Cloth, price 3s. 6d.

The Crowned Hippolytus. Translated from Euripides. With New Poems. Small crown 8vo. Cloth, price 5s.

RODWELL (G. F.), F.R.A.S., F.C.S.

Etna: a History of the Mountain and its Eruptions. With Maps and Illustrations. Square 8vo. Cloth, price 9s.

ROLLESTON (T. W. H.), B.A.

The Encheiridion of Epictetus. Translated from the Greek, with a Preface and Notes. Small crown 8vo. Cloth, price 3s. 6d.

ROSS (Mrs. E.), ("Nelsie Brook").

Daddy's Pet. A Sketch from Humble Life. With Six Illustrations. Royal 16mo. Cloth, price 1s.

SADLER (S. W.), R.N.

The African Cruiser. A Midshipman's Adventures on the West Coast. With Three Illustrations. Second Edition. Crown 8vo. Cloth, price 3s. 6d.

SALTS (Rev. Alfred), LL.D.

Godparents at Confirmation. With a Preface by the Bishop of Manchester. Small crown 8vo. Cloth, limp, price 2s.

SALVATOR (Archduke Ludwig).

Levkosia, the Capital of Cyprus. Crown 8vo. Cloth, price 10s. 6d.

SAMUEL (Sydney Montagu).

Jewish Life in the East. Small crown 8vo. Cloth, price 3s. 6d.

SAUNDERS (John).

Israel Mort, Overman: A Story of the Mine. Cr. 8vo. Price 6s.

Hirell. With Frontispiece. Crown 8vo. Cloth, price 3s. 6d.

Abel Drake's Wife. With Frontispiece. Crown 8vo. Cloth, price 3s. 6d.

SAYCE (Rev. Archibald Henry).

Introduction to the Science of Language. Two vols., large post 8vo. Cloth, price 25s.

SCHELL (Maj. von).

The Operations of the First Army under Gen. von Goeben. Translated by Col. C. H. von Wright. Four Maps. Demy 8vo. Cloth, price 9s.

The Operations of the First Army under Gen. von Steinmetz. Translated by Captain E. O. Hollist. Demy 8vo. Cloth, price 10s. 6d.

SCHELLENDORF (Maj.-Gen. B. von).

The Duties of the General Staff. Translated from the German by Lieutenant Hare. Vol. I. Demy 8vo. Cloth, 10s. 6d.

SCHERFF (Maj. W. von).

Studies in the New Infantry Tactics. Parts I. and II. Translated from the German by Colonel Lumley Graham. Demy 8vo. Cloth, price 7s. 6d.

Scientific Layman. The New Truth and the Old Faith: are they Incompatible? Demy 8vo. Cloth, price 10s. 6d.

SCOONES (W. Baptiste).
Four Centuries of English
Letters. A Selection of 350 Letters
by 150 Writers from the period of the
Paston Letters to the Present Time.
Edited and arranged by. Second
Edition. Large crown 8vo. Cloth,
price 9s.

SCOTT (Leader).
A Nook in the Apennines:
A Summer beneath the Chestnuts.
With Frontispiece, and 27 Illustra-
tions in the Text, chiefly from
Original Sketches. Crown 8vo.
Cloth, price 7s. 6d. Also a Cheap
Edition, price 2s. 6d.

SCOTT (Robert H.).
Weather Charts and Storm
Warnings. Illustrated. Second Edi-
tion. Crown 8vo. Cloth, price 3s. 6d.

Seeking his Fortune, and
other Stories. With Four Illustrations. New and cheaper Edition.
Crown 8vo. Cloth, price 2s. 6d.

SENIOR (N. W.).
Alexis De Tocqueville.
Correspondence and Conversations
with Nassau W. Senior, from 1833 to
1859. Edited by M. C. M. Simpson.
2 vols. Large post 8vo. Cloth, price 21s.

Seven Autumn Leaves from
Fairyland. Illustrated with Nine
Etchings. Square crown 8vo. Cloth,
price 3s. 6d.

SHADWELL (Maj.-Gen.), C.B.
Mountain Warfare. Illustrated by the Campaign of 1799 in
Switzerland. Being a Translation
of the Swiss Narrative compiled from
the Works of the Archduke Charles,
Jomini, and others. Also of Notes
by General H. Dufour on the Campaign of the Valtelline in 1635. With
Appendix, Maps, and Introductory
Remarks. Demy 8vo. Cloth, price 16s.

SHAKSPEARE (Charles).
Saint Paul at Athens:
Spiritual Christianity in Relation to
some Aspects of Modern Thought.
Nine Sermons preached at St. Ste-
phen's Church, Westbourne Park.
With Preface by the Rev. Canon
FARRAR. Crown 8vo. Cloth, price 5s.

SHAW (Major Wilkinson).
The Elements of Modern
Tactics. Practically applied to
English Formations. With Twenty-
five Plates and Maps. Second and
cheaper Edition. Small crown 8vo.
Cloth, price 9s.
. The Second Volume of "Mili-
tary Handbooks for Officers and
Non-commissioned Officers." Edited
by Lieut.-Col. C. B. Brackenbury,
R.A., A.A.G.

SHAW (Flora L.).
Castle Blair: a Story of
Youthful Lives. 2 vols. Crown 8vo.
Cloth, gilt tops, price 12s. Also, an
dition in one vol. Crown 8vo. 6s.

SHELLEY (Lady).
Shelley Memorials from
Authentic Sources. With (now
first printed) an Essay on Christianity by Percy Bysshe Shelley. With
Portrait. Third Edition. Crown
8vo. Cloth, price 5s.

SHERMAN (Gen. W. T.).
Memoirs of General W.
T. Sherman, Commander of the
Federal Forces in the American Civil
War. By Himself. 2 vols. With
Map. Demy 8vo Cloth, price 24s.
Copyright English Edition.

SHILLITO (Rev. Joseph).
Womanhood: its Duties,
Temptations, and Privileges. A Book
for Young Women. Second Edition.
Crown 8vo. Price 3s. 6d.

SHIPLEY (Rev. Orby), M.A.
Principles of the Faith in
Relation to Sin. Topics for
Thought in Times of Retreat.
Eleven Addresses. With an Intro-
duction on the neglect of Dogmatic
Theology in the Church of England,
and a Postscript on his leaving the
Church of England. Demy 8vo.
Cloth, price 12s.

Church Tracts, or Studies
in Modern Problems. By various
Writers. 2 vols. Crown 8vo. Cloth,
price 5s. each.

Sister Augustine, Superior
of the Sisters of Charity at the St.
Johannis Hospital at Bonn. Authorized Translation by Hans Tharau
from the German Memorials of Ama-
lie von Lasaulx. Second edition.
Large crown 8vo. Cloth, price 7s. 6d.

Six Ballads about King Arthur. Crown 8vo. Cloth extra, gilt edges, price 3s. 6d.

SKINNER (James).

Cœlestia : the Manual of St. Augustine. The Latin Text side by side with an English Interpretation, in 36 Odes, with Notes, *and* a plea *for the* Study *of* Mystic Theology. Large crown 8vo. Cloth, price 6s.

SMITH (Edward), M.D., LL.B., F.R.S.

Health and Disease, as In-fluenced by the Daily, Seasonal, and other Cyclical Changes in the Human System. A New Edition. Post 8vo. Cloth, price 7s. 6d.

Practical Dietary for Families, Schools, and the La-bouring Classes. A New Edition. Post 8vo. Cloth, price 3s. 6d.

Tubercular Consumption in its Early and Remediable Stages. Second Edition. Crown 8vo. Cloth, price 6s.

Songs of Two Worlds. By the Author of "The Epic of Hades." Sixth Edition. Complete in one Volume, with Portrait. Fcap. 8vo. Cloth, price 7s. 6d.

Songs for Music. By Four Friends. Square crown 8vo. Cloth, price 5s. Containing songs by Reginald A. Gatty, Stephen H. Gatty, Greville J. Chester, and Juliana Ewing.

SPEDDING (James).

Evenings with a Reviewer; or, Bacon and Macaulay. With a Prefatory Notice by G. S. VENABLES, Q.C. 3 vols. Demy 8vo. Cloth, price 18s.

Reviews and Discussions, Literary, Political, and His-torical, not relating to Bacon. Demy 8vo. Cloth, price 12s. 6d.

STAPFER (Paul).

Shakspeare and Classical Antiquity : Greek and Latin Anti-

STAPFER (Paul)—*continued.*
quity as presented in Shakspeare's Plays. Translated by Emily J. Carey. Large post 8vo. Cloth, price 12s.

St. Bernard on the Love of God. Translated by Marianne Caroline and Coventry Patmore. Cloth extra, gilt top, price 4s. 6d.

STEDMAN (Edmund Clarence).

Lyrics and Idylls. With other Poems. Crown 8vo. Cloth, price 7s. 6d.

STEPHENS (Archibald John), LL.D.

The Folkestone Ritual Case. The Substance of the Argu-ment delivered before the Judicial Committee of the Privy Council. On behalf of the Respondents. Demy 8vo. Cloth, price 6s.

STEVENSON (Robert Louis).

Virginibus, Puerisque, and other Papers. Crown 8vo. Cloth, price 6s.

STEVENSON (Rev. W. F.).

Hymns for the Church and Home. Selected and Edited by the Rev. W. Fleming Stevenson.

The most complete Hymn Book published.

The Hymn Book consists of Three Parts :—I. For Public Worship.—II. For Family and Private Worship.—III. For Children.

. *Published in various forms and prices, the latter ranging from 8d. to 6s. Lists and full particulars will be furnished on application to the Publishers.*

STOCKTON (Frank R.).

A Jolly Fellowship. With 20 Illustrations. Crown 8vo. Cloth, price 5s.

STORR (Francis), and TURNER Hawes).

Canterbury Chimes; or, Chaucer Tales retold to Children. With Illustrations from the Elles-mere MS. Extra Fcap. 8vo. Cloth, price 3s. 6d.

Strecker-Wishcenus's Organic Chemistry. Translated and edited with extensive additions by W. R. HODGKINSON, Ph. D., and A. J. GREENWAY, F.I C. Demy 8vo. Cloth, price 21s.

STRETTON (Hesba).
David Lloyd's Last Will. With Four Illustrations. Royal 16mo., price 2s. 6d.

The Wonderful Life. Thirteenth Thousand. Fcap. 8vo. Cloth, price 2s. 6d.

Through a Needle's Eye : a Story. Crown 8vo. Cloth, price 6s.

STUBBS (Lieut.-Colonel F. W.)
The Regiment of Bengal Artillery. The History of its Organization, Equipment, and War Services. Compiled from Published Works, Official Records, and various Private Sources. With numerous Maps and Illustrations. 2 vols. Demy 8vo. Cloth, price 32s.

STUMM (Lieut. Hugo), German Military Attaché to the Khivan Expedition.

Russia's advance Eastward. Based on the Official Reports of. Translated by Capt. C. E. H. VINCENT. With Map. Crown 8vo. Cloth, price 6s.

SULLY (James), M.A.
Sensation and Intuition. Demy 8vo. Second Edition. Cloth, price 10s. 6d.
Pessimism : a History and a Criticism. Demy 8vo. Price 14s.

Sunnyland Stories. By the Author of "Aunt Mary's Bran Pie." Illustrated. Small 8vo. Cloth, price 3s. 6d

Sweet Silvery Sayings of Shakespeare. Crown 8vo. Cloth gilt, price 7s. 6d.

SYME (David).
Outlines of an Industrial Science. Second Edition. Crown 8vo. Cloth, price 6s.

SYME (David)—*continued.*
Representative Government in England. Its Faults and Failures. Large crown 8vo. Cloth, price 6s.

Tales from Ariosto. Retold for Children, by a Lady. With three illustrations. Crown 8vo. Cloth, price 4s. 6d.

TAYLOR (Algernon).
Guienne. Notes of an Autumn Tour. Crown 8vo. Cloth, price 4s 6d.

TAYLOR (Sir H.).
Works Complete. Author's Edition, in 5 vols. Crown 8vo. Cloth, price 6s. each.
Vols. I. to III. containing the Poetical Works, Vols. IV. and V. the Prose Works.

TAYLOR (Col. Meadows), C.S.I., M.R.I.A.
A Noble Queen : a Romance of Indian History. New Edition. With Frontispiece. Crown 8vo. Cloth. Price 6s.
Seeta. New Edition with frontispiece. Crown 8vo. Cloth, price 6s.
Tippoo Sultaun : a Tale of the Mysore War. New Edition with Frontispiece. Crown 8vo. Cloth, price 6s.
Ralph Darnell. New Edition. With Frontispiece. Crown 8vo. Cloth, price 6s.
The Confessions of a Thug. New Edition. With Frontispiece. Crown 8vo. Cloth, price 6s.
Tara : a Mahratta Tale. New Edition. With Frontispiece. Crown 8vo. Cloth, price 6s.

TENNYSON (Alfred).
The Imperial Library Edition. Complete in 7 vols. Demy 8vo. Cloth, price £3 13s. 6d. ; in Roxburgh binding, £4 7s. 6d.
Author's Edition. Complete in 7 Volumes. With Frontispieces. Crown 8vo. Cloth, price 43s. 6d. Roxburgh half morocco, price 54s.

TENNYSON (Alfred)—*continued.*

Cabinet Edition, in 13 vols. with Frontispieces. Fcap. 8vo. Cloth, price 2s. 6d. each, or complete in cloth box, price 35s.

** Each volume in the above editions may be had separately.

The Royal Edition. With 26 Illustrations and Portrait. Cloth extra, bevelled boards, gilt leaves. Price 21s.

The Guinea Edition. In 14 vols., neatly bound and enclosed in box. Cloth, price 21s. French morocco or parchment, price 31s. 6d.

The Shilling Edition of the Poetical and Dramatic Works, in 12 vols., pocket size. Price 1s. each.

The Crown Edition [the 113th thousand], strongly bound in cloth, price 6s. Cloth, extra gilt leaves, price 7s. 6d. Roxburgh, half morocco, price 8s. 6d.

** Can also be had in a variety of other bindings.

Original Editions :

Ballads and other Poems. Fcap. 8vo. Cloth, price 5s.

The Lover's Tale. (Now for the first time published.) Fcap. 8vo. Cloth, 3s. 6d.

Poems. Small 8vo. Cloth, price 6s.

Maud, and other Poems. Small 8vo. Cloth, price 3s. 6d.

The Princess. Small 8vo. Cloth, price 3s. 6d.

Idylls of the King. Small 8vo. Cloth, price 5s.

Idylls of the King. Complete. Small 8vo. Cloth, price 6s.

The Holy Grail, and other Poems. Small 8vo. Cloth, price 4s. 6d.

Gareth and Lynette. Small 8vo. Cloth, price 3s.

Enoch Arden, &c. Small 8vo. Cloth, price 3s. 6d.

TENNYSON (Alfred)—*continued.*

In Memoriam. Small 8vo. Cloth, price 4s.

Queen Mary. A Drama. New Edition. Crown 8vo. Cloth, price 6s.

Harold. A Drama. Crown 8vo. Cloth, price 6s.

Selections from Tennyson's Works. Super royal 16mo. Cloth, price 3s. 6d. Cloth gilt extra, price 4s.

Songs from Tennyson's Works. Super royal 16mo. Cloth extra, price 3s. 6d.

Also a cheap edition. 16mo. Cloth, price 2s. 6d.

Idylls of the King, and other Poems. Illustrated by Julia Margaret Cameron. 2 vols. Folio. Half-bound morocco, cloth sides, price £6 6s. each.

Tennyson for the Young and for Recitation. Specially arranged. Fcap. 8vo. Price 1s. 6d.

Tennyson Birthday Book. Edited by Emily Shakespear. 32mo. Cloth limp, 2s. ; cloth extra, 3s.

** A superior edition, printed in red and black, on antique paper, specially prepared. Small crown 8vo. Cloth extra, gilt leaves, price 5s. ; and in various calf and morocco bindings.

Songs Set to Music, by various Composers. Edited by W. G. Cusins. Dedicated by express permission to Her Majesty the Queen. Royal 4to. Cloth extra, gilt leaves, price 21s., or in half-morocco, price 25s.

An Index to "In Memoriam." Price 2s.

THOMAS (Moy).
A Fight for Life. With Frontispiece. Crown 8vo. Cloth, price 3s. 6d.

THOMPSON (Alice C.).
Preludes. A Volume of Poems. Illustrated by Elizabeth Thompson (Painter of "The Roll Call"). 8vo. Cloth, price 7s. 6d.

THOMSON (J. Turnbull).
Social Problems; or, an Inquiry into the Law of Influences. With Diagrams. Demy 8vo. Cloth, price 10s. 6d.

THRING (Rev. Godfrey), B.A.
Hymns and Sacred Lyrics. Fcap. 8vo. Cloth, price 3s. 6d.

TODHUNTER (Dr. J.)
Forest Songs. Small crown 8vo. Cloth, 3s. 6d.
The True Tragedy of Rienzi. A Drama.
A Study of Shelley. Crown 8vo. Cloth, price 7s.
Alcestis : A Dramatic Poem. Extra fcap. 8vo. Cloth, price 5s.
Laurella; and other Poems. Crown 8vo. Cloth, price 6s. 6d.
Translations from Dante, Petrarch, Michael Angelo, and Vittoria Colonna. Fcap. 8vo. Cloth, price 7s. 6d.

TURNER (Rev. C. Tennyson).
Sonnets, Lyrics, and Translations. Crown 8vo. Cloth, price 4s. 6d.
Collected Sonnets, Old and New. With Prefatory Poem by Alfred Tennyson; also some Marginal Notes by S. T. Coleridge, and a Critical Essay by James Spedding. Fcap. 8vo. Cloth, price 7s. 6d.

TWINING (Louisa).
Recollections of Workhouse Visiting and Management during twenty-five years. Small crown 8vo. Cloth, price 3s. 6d.

UPTON (Major R. D.).
Gleanings from the Desert of Arabia. Large post 8vo. Cloth, price 10s. 6d.

VAUGHAN (H. Halford).
New Readings and Renderings of Shakespeare's Tragedies. 2 vols. Demy 8vo. Cloth, price 25s.

VIATOR (Vacuus).
Flying South. Recollections of France and its Littoral. Small crown 8vo. Cloth, price 3s. 6d.

VILLARI (Prof.).
Niccolo Machiavelli and His Times. Translated by Linda Villari. 2 vols. Large post 8vo. Cloth, price 24s.

VINCENT (Capt. C. E. H.).
Elementary Military Geography, Reconnoitring, and Sketching. Square crown 8vo. Cloth, price 2s. 6d.

VYNER (Lady Mary).
Every day a Portion. Adapted from the Bible and the Prayer Book. Square crown 8vo. Cloth extra, price 5s.

WALDSTEIN (Charles), Ph. D.
The Balance of Emotion and Intellect: An Essay Introductory to the Study of Philosophy. Crown 8vo. Cloth, price 6s.

WALLER (Rev. C. B.)
The Apocalypse, Reviewed under the Light of the Doctrine of the Unfolding Ages and the Restitution of all Things. Demy 8vo. Cloth, price 12s.

WALSHE (Walter Hayle), M.D.
Dramatic Singing Physiologically Estimated. Crown 8vo. Cloth, price 3s. 6d.

WALTERS (Sophia Lydia).
The Brook : A Poem. Small crown 8vo. Cloth, price 3s. 6d.
A Dreamer's Sketch Book. With Twenty-one Illustrations. Fcap. 4to. Cloth, price 12s. 6d.

WATERFIELD, W.
Hymns for Holy Days and Seasons. 32mo. Cloth, price 1s. 6d.

WATSON (Sir Thomas), Bart., M.D.
The Abolition of Zymotic Diseases, and of other similar enemies of Mankind. Small crown 8vo. Cloth, price 3s. 6d.

WAY (A.), M.A.
The Odes of Horace Literally Translated in Metre. Fcap. 8vo. Cloth, price 2s.

WEBSTER (Augusta).
Disguises. A Drama. Small crown 8vo. Cloth, price 5s.

WEDMORE (Frederick).
The Masters of Genre Painting. With sixteen illustrations. Large crown 8vo. Cloth, price 7s. 6d.

WHEWELL (William), D.D.
His Life and Selections from his Correspondence. By Mrs. Stair Douglas. With Portrait. Demy 8vo. Cloth, price 21s.

WHITAKER (Florence).
Christy's Inheritance. A London Story. Illustrated. Royal 16mo. Cloth, price 1s. 6d.

WHITE (A. D.), LL.D.
Warfare of Science. With Prefatory Note by Professor Tyndall. Second Edition. Crown 8vo. Cloth, price 3s. 6d.

WHITNEY (Prof. W. D.)
Essentials of English Grammar for the Use of Schools. Crown 8vo. Cloth, price 3s. 6d.

WICKSTEED (P. H.).
Dante: Six Sermons. Crown 8vo. Cloth, price 5s.

WILKINS (William).
Songs of Study. Crown 8vo. Cloth, price 6s.

WILLIAMS (Rowland), D.D.
Stray Thoughts from his Note-Books. Edited by his Widow. Crown 8vo. Cloth, price 3s. 6d.

Psalms, Litanies, Counsels and Collects for Devout Persons. Edited by his Widow. Crown 8vo. Cloth, price 3s. 6d.

WILLIS (R.), M.D.
Servetus and Calvin : a Study of an Important Epoch in the Early History of the Reformation. 8vo. Cloth, price 16s.

William Harvey. A History of the Discovery of the Circulation of the Blood. With a Portrait of Harvey, after Faithorne. Demy 8vo. Cloth, price 14s.

WILSON (Sir Erasmus).
Egypt of the Past. With Illustrations in the Text. Crown 8vo. Cloth, price 12s.

WILSON (H. Schütz).
The Tower and Scaffold. Large fcap. 8vo. Price 1s.

Within Sound of the Sea. By the Author of " Blue Roses," "Vera," &c. Fourth Edition in one vol. with frontispiece. Price 6s.

WOLLSTONECRAFT (Mary).
Letters to Imlay. With a Preparatory Memoir by C. Kegan Paul, and two Portraits in *eau forte* by Anna Lea Merritt. Crown 8vo. Cloth, price 6s.

WOLTMANN (Dr. Alfred), and WOERMANN (Dr. Karl).
History of Painting in Antiquity and the Middle Ages. Edited by Sidney Colvin. With numerous illustrations. Medium 8vo. Cloth, price 28s. ; cloth, bevelled boards, gilt leaves, price 30s.

WOOD (Major-General J. Creighton).
Doubling the Consonant. Small crown 8vo. Cloth, price 1s. 6d.

Word was made Flesh. Short Family Readings on the Epistles for each Sunday of the Christian Year. Demy 8vo. Cloth, price 10s. 6d.

Wren (Sir Christopher) ; his Family and his Times. With Original Letters, and a Discourse on Architecture hitherto unpublished. By Lucy Phillimore. Demy 8vo. With Portrait, price 14s.

WRIGHT (Rev. David), M.A.
Waiting for the Light, and other Sermons. Crown 8vo. Cloth, price 6s.

YOUMANS (Eliza A.).
An Essay on the Culture of the Observing Powers of Children. Crown 8vo. Cloth, price 2s. 6d.

First Book of Botany. With 300 Engravings. Crown 8vo. Cloth, price 2s. 6d.

YOUMANS (Edward L.), M.D.
A Class Book of Chemistry. With 200 Illustrations. Crown 8vo. Cloth, price 5s.

www.ingramcontent.com/pod-product-compliance
Lightning Source LLC
Chambersburg PA
CBHW020853020726
47497CB00005B/1393